RAVEN'S FLIGHT

By Diane Silvey

RAINCOAST BOOKS

Vancouver

Raincoast Books acknowledges the ongoing support of The Canada Council; the British Columbia Ministry of Small Business, Tourism and Culture through the BC Arts Council; and the Government of Canada through the Book Publishing Industry Development Program (BPIDP).

First published in 2000 by

Raincoast Books
9050 Shaughnessy Street
Vancouver, B.C.
V6P 6E5
(604) 323-7100

www.raincoast.com

Edited by Joy Gugeler
Cover art by Thomas Anfield
Cover design by Les Smith
Typeset by Bamboo & Silk Design Inc.

1 2 3 4 5 6 7 8 9 10

CANADIAN CATALOGUING IN PUBLICATION DATA
 Silvey, Diane.
 Raven's flight
 ISBN 1-55192-344-0
 I. Title.
 PS8587.I278R38 2000   jC813'.54   C00-910915-3
 PZ7.S58845Ra 2000

Printed and bound in Canada

*For all those who wanted to write home
but the shadows got in the way*

ONE

Raven shuffled the letters on the kitchen table like a deck of cards, hungry for any scrap of news from her sister, Marcie. Marcie had left Egmont to look for a job in Vancouver several weeks ago and had sent only cryptic messages assuring her parents she was "surviving" since. She had not shared specific details about her job or how she was making ends meet; after several unsatisfactory phone calls, the family began to suspect she was keeping something from them.

Marcie had made the decision to move to the city, rooming with her 19-year-old cousin, Rita, as a way to escape the small community on B.C.'s Sunshine Coast, but her perception of the city had been built on a flimsy foundation of rumour, gossip and dream. Marcie had been sure she would find work that would finance a new life: her own car, apartment, wardrobe, plenty of spending money and maybe even a boyfriend.

But it was a sunny Sunday morning, so Raven brushed aside her worry in favour of the distraction of work. She stuffed her gloves, tie wire and a machete (checking to make sure it was locked in its case) in her knapsack and set off across the field to the woods. The overgrown and weedy path soon became too difficult to navigate. She unsheathed the machete and grasped it by its hilt. She swung it in wide sweeping arcs so the tall grass met the sharp blade with a *swish* and quickly cleared a trail up the hill. At the peak of the hill lay a campground, but the discovery of tainted drinking water in its well last season meant it was now virtually deserted.

Raven entered the campground from the north end and resumed hiking toward the salal berry patch. Her family had picked salal in this spot for as long as she could remember; she and her favourite aunt, Edna, had passed hours here on the weekends, their nimble fingers plucking handfuls of the salal bush for sale to a wholesaler, who in turn had sold it to the florist in town, its dark green leaves providing a flourish in bouquets and centrepieces.

After several hours of picking, Raven gathered all the salal bush she could carry, bound it in bundles and hoisted it on her back. She adjusted her grandmother's old hand-woven tumpline across her shoulders and took the south trail home along an old logging road.

Rounding a huge stump she came upon a large black truck with oversized wheels parked to the side of the trail; small sacklike pouches were spread out on the ground behind the tailgate. The remains of a female bear lay slit open on the ground next to them; the scene resembled a grotesque sacrificial offering. Raven knew the high demand for bear gall bladders made poaching a very lucrative business. One alone could fetch over $2,000. Unscrupulous hunters illegally sold the fist-sized sacs to smugglers who transported them to the black market in Hong Kong, where they were worth their weight in gold for use in traditional Chinese medicinal remedies. The slaughter was perpetuated by the hunters' greed and by the buyers' ignorance and superstition.

Raven's grandmother had raised her to appreciate their own traditional ways, to respect not only the bear, but all living things. She had been taught that if an animal was to be killed, the hunter must first prepare ritually, then explain to the animal why it was needed. Her grandmother had warned her that no one should ever waste any part of an animal, as this would be both careless and disrespectful. If these practices were not followed, the animal would not offer itself to the hunter.

She heard male voices nearby and, assuming they were the hunters, Raven dropped her bundle of salal in her haste to avoid being seen. The noise alerted them to her presence and they immediately gave chase. She raced toward the beach trail, sure they were following and gaining ground. Raven heard heavy breathing and the thud of footsteps several feet behind her.

"Leave her. She won't be able to identify us or the truck and we have to deliver this load tonight," Raven heard one of the men yell from further off in the distance. She ducked behind a tree and watched as the other man angrily stomped up the path. He flung the truck door open so hard it nearly ripped off the hinges. He jumped into the front seat, cursing, and punched the dashboard with such force his clenched fist left an indentation. Meanwhile, his partner had gathered the pouches and stored them in the back of the truck. In a hurry to meet his buyer, he pumped the accelerator and the truck roared off, dirt spewing in a fan behind its spinning tires. Raven breathed a sigh of relief and headed home.

When she got back to the house, her dad called from the other room, "Raven, is that you?"

Raven replied with a rush of words, anxious to explain the whole story about the poachers. When she had, she asked her father to call the conservation officer and report the illegal activity in the woods.

"We'll do that in a minute, but right now we have a more pressing matter to deal with. Marcie is missing," her father said.

"Missing? What's happened?" Raven said, alarmed.

"We don't know. Your cousin Rita phoned the store and left a message saying no one had seen or heard from your sister in days," he said, worriedly.

"Someone has to go to the city and look for her," Raven blurted.

"There's barely enough money for food for you and your brothers, let alone enough to go to the city," he explained.

"I have money. We can use that," Raven answered. She had earned extra money picking salal or taking babysitting jobs on weekends while she went to high school. Half of the money she earned was set aside for university and the rest she put into the family pot for groceries. Raven studied hard to keep up her grade point average in hopes of a university scholarship to UBC. If she completed the law program, she would be the first in her village to acquire a university degree.

"We can't use your money," he said, adamant that her savings be kept for tuition.

"We have no choice. I can always put off going for another year if I have to," Raven insisted. "Which one of us will go?"

"Your mother can't go. She can't leave the baby," her father said, his brow furrowed. "And I can't go now or I'd lose my job at the fishery."

"I'll go," Raven offered.

"You can't go. You're too young to be in the big city by yourself," he said as fast as the words left her lips.

"I have to go. I'll be all right. I can look after myself. Besides, I can stay with Rita; she's an adult. If Marcie isn't there, there will be a spare bed. I'll have a place to stay and I'll be in the area where she likely disappeared — it's my best chance of finding her. Rita will look out for me," Raven pleaded.

"I haven't seen Rita in a long time. I don't even know what she does or what the neighbourhood is like — the area may not be safe. How do we know we could trust her to look after you?"

"We don't have a choice. No one else can go. I couldn't live with myself if I didn't do *something*. I'm sure she wouldn't mind if I stayed with her," Raven coaxed.

"I could go over to the store and call her from there. If it's all right with Rita, you can go, but you have to listen to her. Vancouver is not a safe place. I don't even want you going on the city bus alone. You have to be supervised."

A few moments later her father grabbed his coat and headed toward the beach. Raven and her two younger brothers, Allan and Tim, scampered after him, eager for a ride in the fishing boat. Her father held the boat steady as they jumped in, checked to make sure their life jackets were fastened properly and headed toward the store on the far shore. Fifteen minutes later he tied the boat to the dock's mooring post and walked toward Frank's General Store. Raven's brothers' hoots and hollers were more than enough to announce company was coming. As the bells above the door rang, Frank, the owner, came out to the counter.

"Hey, Jim. How you been keeping?" Frank asked.

"I've been better, Frank, but hanging in there. You?" Jim replied. The two boys already had their noses pressed against the candy display case.

"My arthritis is acting up, but other than that I'm fine. Looks like these two youngsters have their hearts set on something. What will it be boys?" Frank chuckled softly. He had been a friend of the family for years.

"Licorice sticks!" they yelled in chorus.

Frank passed each of them a long stalk of black licorice.

"Why don't you sit outside on the front steps with Raven? I won't be long," their father instructed. "Frank, I need to call my niece in Vancouver."

"Sure. What's the number?"

He pulled a folded piece of paper out of his pocket and placed the long-distance call with the operator.

The phone in the second-floor hallway of Rita's rooming house rang and rang, but finally someone answered and knocked on Rita's door to tell her she had a call. Rita got on the line, her voice wary and low.

"Rita, is that you? How are you? It's your uncle Jim," Raven's father said.

"I'm fine. I guess you got my message this afternoon. Are you coming to town?" Rita answered.

"Actually, I'm phoning to ask if Raven can come and stay with you for a few days."

"I have to work, but if she doesn't mind looking after herself until I get home…," she hedged.

"I think she'll be all right if she stays close by and is only out by day. I can check in on her at this number. I'll put her on the bus tomorrow."

"When will she get in to the depot?" Rita asked unenthusiastically.

"The bus gets arrives at 10 p.m. tomorrow night. Not a great schedule, but it's the only one that works with the ferry."

Rita wrote the instructions on a notepad. "I'll meet her at the station. I could use the help with the rent now that Marcie's not around. The landlord collects it weekly."

"She'll have some spending money and enough to cover the days she's there. Hopefully, both of my girls will be home soon. We're trying not to worry. Call as soon as she gets there. OK?"

"Don't worry, I'll take good care of her," Rita said, hanging up. She doodled over the instructions on the notepad. The message read May 9th, but was that 10 or 11 p.m.?

Raven was quiet on the boat trip back, suddenly worried she had spoken too soon, too confidently.

Back at the house, she and her father reached under her bed and took out the old safety deposit box. Raven walked over to the dresser and opened the top drawer, reached in and pulled out a key. Opening the box, her father took out a stack of papers, photos of the family and a tin can with Raven's name on it. It held $2,345, the sum of what she had saved.

"How much do you think I'll need?" Raven asked.

"It's hard to say. You won't need much for your accommodation and hopefully Rita's got food in the apartment, so it will just be transportation money and an emergency stash if something comes up. It's better not to take too much in case it gets stolen, lost or tempts you to spend foolishly," he said.

"I'll take $200," Raven decided, hoping she would find Marcie before she had gone through too much of her hard-earned savings.

That night, she packed her knapsack with clothes

and toiletry articles. She lay in bed trying to picture life in the city. Marcie had talked about it with stars in her eyes — parties, clubs, shopping, movies — all the things they didn't have in their small fishing village. She had wanted independence and a chance to be on her own in a new place, but what price had she paid for freedom? Raven closed her eyes and tried not to imagine the worst. She'd just have to wait and see.

The next morning Raven and her father took their fishing boat to the ferry terminal at Earls Cove. They tied up at the small dock and walked up the road to flag down the bus when it drove off the ferry from Saltery Bay. A few minutes later, the bus pulled over onto the gravel.

Raven hugged her father before boarding and bought a ticket to Vancouver from the driver, who punched it and waved her down the aisle to find a vacant seat. The bus made several stops en route, including the Sechelt bus terminal, where she got off to stretch her legs. Next stop was Gibsons and then the Langdale ferry terminal; the ferry was just pulling into sight.

Even though she had relatives in Vancouver, she had only been to the city when she was very small and could barely remember it now. Her parents had wanted her to be brought up according to their traditions and thought that the city schools and neighbourhoods would distract her from the values they believed were important. She hadn't envied what other kids had at the time, but she had been curious. Now, under the worst circumstances, she was going to find out if she had been missing anything. Despite her nervousness about what lay ahead, the steady hum of the tires almost lulled her to sleep.

No wonder Marcie loves the city, Raven thought to herself, looking out the window at the bright city lights, spread out like a canvas of twinkling diamonds against the night sky. As the bus continued across the Lion's Gate bridge, through Stanley Park and along Georgia Street, passengers got on and off, so familiar with the route they read newspapers and books rather than watched the traffic. Raven sat up straight, anxious to arrive.

The bus crossed the Georgia viaduct and headed east into a part of the city with boarded-up buildings, hotels and bars. The Cobalt Hotel had more than 30 motorcycles parked in formation. Across the street, next to the American Hotel, two telephone receivers dangled uselessly from cables, their wires ripped out. The bus continued up Main Street, then turned left and left again into the Vancouver bus depot.

It was 10 p.m. The depot was deserted except for the few passengers getting off the bus. Where was Rita? Perhaps she was inside, waiting. Raven walked inside and searched the lobby. She was nowhere to be seen. What now? She searched her backpack for her cousin's phone number, dialled and waited. It rang and rang. She would give Rita another hour before trying to find her place on her own. She sat down on a wooden bench facing the large clock in the middle of the depot. Every time someone walked through the door, she looked up expectantly. She waited until 11 p.m. and then tried the phone number again. Nothing.

Raven walked back outside to the bus, where the driver was still sorting freight. She decided to get directions and take the chance that Rita would be there to let her in. She must have written down the arrival time incorrectly.

"Can I help you, Miss?" the driver inquired.

"Yes, thanks. I need directions to my cousin's place," Raven responded.

The bus driver looked at the address on the paper Raven showed him and frowned. "Anyone meeting you?" he hedged.

"My cousin was supposed to, but she's not here, so I thought I'd walk," she replied.

"Well, you'd better be careful. That's a bad area," the driver warned. "Go through this building, then straight out the main doors and through the park; make sure you stay in the middle of the path and don't stop or talk to anyone. On the far side of the park is Main Street. When you reach it, turn right. The hotel's a couple of blocks down the street," he said.

"Thank you. I'll find it," Raven answered, a little unsure of her bearings, but determined nonetheless.

Raven walked through the building, still searching for her cousin's familiar face, out the main automatic doors to where yellow taxicabs waited idly for fares and finally along the path, keeping her eyes focused straight ahead until she spotted Main Street. Just before she reached the curb, the sound of a deep cough emerged from the shadows, startling her. She sprinted toward the lights and traffic, not bothering to look back.

Over her shoulder she heard someone's hoarse voice baiting her, "Hey kid, why don't you come and have a drink?"

"Yeah, come and have a snort," jeered another.

She ignored them and felt inside her jacket pocket for the paper with her cousin's address printed on it. If only she were there already....

TWO

R aven walked along Main nervously checking the numbers above each doorway. Her hands shook. She looked up at a dilapidated building with the street number dangling off a shingle. There must be some mistake. This neglected old dump couldn't be where her sister lived. Marcie's letters home told of how well she was doing and how much she loved her modern new apartment. This was a rundown hotel that rented rooms by the week — not really an apartment at all. The sign out front read: NO DRUGS. NO PARTIES. NO VISITORS AFTER 10 P.M.

It was after 10 p.m. now, but she had to take a chance Rita would let her in before a landlord spotted her. Raven tried the tarnished doorknob to see if it was locked, but as she turned it, it almost fell off in her hands. The lock had been jimmied so often the landlord must have given up trying to fix it. Raven opened the door cautiously. The rusty hinges creaked. It took her eyes a few seconds to adjust to the dim interior.

The stairwell lay in total darkness. A burnt-out light bulb dangled haphazardly from a long, frayed cord above the stairs. She made her way gingerly up the lopsided stairs toward a light from one of the upstairs rooms. Something moved furtively in the shadows. A rat raced past her and down the stairs. Raven shuddered, took a deep breath and continued.

At the top landing she began looking for her sister's room, number seven. She located it and knocked on the door. A hollow echo resounded along the hall.

A door down the hall opened and a scruffy, middle-aged man peered out. "There's nobody there, sweet thing. Why don't you come and wait here until they get back?" he wheezed. He wore a soiled undershirt and baggy pants held up with a cord. He reeked of alcohol, even several feet away, and he swayed a little before retreating into his room.

In desperation, she knocked louder on the door. It opened a crack and a tough-looking man in his 20s peered out at her.

"What you want, kid?" he sneered.

"My, my sister. Or Rita, my cousin," Raven stuttered.

"Yeah, well she ain't here, so get lost," he snarled, shutting the door.

"No, wait. My sister Marcie lives here," Raven protested.

Suddenly, the door swung open. Rita stood in the

doorway. "Hey, kid. We didn't know it was you. Can't be too careful nowadays," she quipped as she winked knowingly at the man beside her. "Don't mind Ted. He's just hung over after hanging out with Christie last night. Feelin' a bit rough, aren't you Teddy boy?"

Ted sat on the edge of a chair. His body rocked, and his legs vibrated rapidly. He clasped his knees to try to still their violent trembling. "I need a hit bad. Hurry up. Let's get going," Ted snarled.

Raven wondered why Ted wanted to go out again if he felt so bad. "Have you heard from Marcie?" Raven asked hopefully.

"Nope. Haven't seen or heard from her in days. We made some inquiries, but nobody's got a clue. Sorry you had to walk over by yourself; we were just getting ready to go over to the station to meet you," she said matter-of-factly, shrugging her shoulders.

"First thing in the morning, I'll start searching for her. Someone must have seen her, must have a lead," Raven hoped.

"I've got to work now, like I said on the phone, and Ted and I are moving out of this dump in three days, so you'll have to too. You can't stay in the city by yourself and there'll be new tenants moving in anyway. Your sister's bed is over in the corner. You can sleep there tonight," she yelled over her shoulder as she and Ted left, slamming the door behind them.

Rita had definitely changed since Raven had last seen her. She seemed tougher, a bit "strung out," and what kind of work did she do at this hour anyway?

Raven didn't think much of her friend Ted — maybe, as her parents had worried, she'd "fallen in with the wrong crowd."

Raven sat on her sister's bed and ran her hand over the threadbare patchwork quilt, her grandmother's handiwork. Marcie used to sit on this very quilt at home and write in her diary, usually when she was upset about something; sometimes she read it aloud to Raven.

That gave her an idea. Raven began shuffling papers and objects around looking for a book that might be Marcie's diary. When she searched under the mattress, her fingers found a diary with a small gold lock on one side. The key was nowhere in sight. Raven glanced at a pile of loose papers lying in the middle of the table. She lifted a few of them and found cookie crumbs and…a brown pill-shaped…something. It had a strange sheen and appeared to be moving. Suddenly, the egg case split and a mob of tiny brown cockroaches crawled out of their shell. She backed away from the table, screaming. When she calmed down, still queasy, she grabbed a glass for a drink of water, but it too was dirty. She wanted to find something to kill the bugs, but everything she touched was disgusting and the bugs had crawled for cover under the floorboards by now anyway.

The room contained a sink, an old fridge, two saggy beds, a table and two rickety chairs. Its cracked linoleum floor and peeling walls made it feel even less welcoming — some apartment. Empty beer bottles and cans lay strewn about. Raven opened the cupboard over the sink, but she slammed the door shut before she could identify the shapes scurrying in the dark. How could she spend the night here with rats and filthy bugs crawling everywhere?

She'd leave the lights on and perch on the edge of Marcie's bed with a big shoe and a spray can of RAID she'd seen in the bathroom — tomorrow she'd try to clean up a bit. She grabbed the blankets, shaking them furiously, then checked under the pillow. There lay the key for the diary; perhaps it would also be the key to discovering the circumstances that led to Marcie's disappearance.

She flipped through the pages looking for the last entry. It was weeks ago. Marcie had faithfully called home every weekend, at first, then she had resorted to just dropping short notes in the mail, but none of what she had said bore any resemblance to these entries.

Dear Diary   Tuesday April 2
I have arrived. This is the beginning of a new life for me. The sky is the limit. First I'll get a good job and then rent my own apartment. I can hardly sleep I'm so excited.

Dear Diary   Wednesday April 3
Had little success finding a job today, but I'm sure tomorrow will be different. I love the streets, the neon lights, the excitement.

Dear Diary   *Thursday April 4*

I applied for other jobs today, but they all require more experience than I have. I tell them that though I didn't graduate from college, I'm willing to learn and work my way to the top. It doesn't look good.

I met some kids today. They're really cool. They hang out on the street corner and smoke and seem to know the city like the backs of their hands. They've offered to show me around and introduce me to somebody who may be able to get me a job — no experience necessary.

Dear Diary   *Friday April 5*

I went for my first ride in a taxicab today. One of the girls got a call on her pager. She said she had to make a run uptown and asked if I wanted to tag along. I couldn't believe it when the fare came to $14! She gave the driver $20 and told him to keep the change. I wouldn't have even earned the tip, $6, for a night of babysitting back home.

Dear Diary   *Saturday April 6*

I didn't have time to look for a job today. My new friends said, "Why bother? There's no jobs out there anyway." Hanging out at Hastings and Main is where it's at. They introduced me to the head guy, Lonnie. He told me he had a friend in the entertainment business that would keep an eye out for a job. I like sitting around with them better than pounding the pavement anyway. I realize this is what it's all about...being where the action is.

Dear Diary   Sunday April 7
    I think I'm falling for him. I've seen Lonnie twice now and he is so, so...good looking. I'm sure he likes me in the same way, except that he has a girlfriend. I don't know what he sees in her. She's really skinny and her hair is scraggly. Anyway, he asked me out for lunch tomorrow. I guess if he really cared about her he wouldn't be flirting with me, so it can't be that serious.

Dear Diary   Monday April 8
    Lonnie offered to buy me some new clothes, said maybe soon I'd be making enough money for a car of my own! He said I was part of the family now and deserved to have the same luxuries the other girls had. What a great guy! When we passed a street vendor, he stopped and bought me a red rose. What next?

Dear Diary   Monday April 15
    As I walked past Oppenheimer Park tonight, I swear I sensed someone, or something, slinking behind me. I could feel it, but I couldn't see it. As I walked faster, its footsteps quickened to keep pace with mine. Terrified, I raced all the way

home. *My hands were shaking so badly I could hardly fit the key in the lock. I yanked the door open, slammed it shut behind me and shot the deadbolt into place. My breathing was shallow, my heart was pounding and my hands were cold and clammy. Safe, safe. But for how long? When I crept toward the window and carefully lifted the blind to peer into the darkness, my eyes detected a flicker of light. There it was again: blue light, an animal's shadow, a coyote flitting through the dark. A chill. Cold, so very, very cold.*

Dear Diary   *Wednesday April 17*
   Having trouble sleeping. I feel so restless, so tired. I'm afraid to shut my eyes. It's getting stronger and stronger...must tell J.L. He will know what to do. The pain is so intense I can't sleep, can't eat. I'm losing control. Help me take the pain away....

Dear Diary   *Thursday April 18*
   It came to me last night. I reached out. I almost touched it. I felt the pain lesson. J.L. says I should stay away. It's addictive. He must be jealous. I can't trust him anymore. I want to write, but the shadows get in the way. Come to me....

Dear Diary   *Monday April 22*
   I dreamt I was sitting in the dark, crying and enveloped in an ominous blue light. A blue coyote

*took form before my eyes — a spirit animal?
No, it couldn't be, besides, I would have had to
prepare ritually before entering a vision quest. It
was an omen from a darker realm. In this place
there were lights, the sound of trains shuttling to
and fro, bells ringing, the gentle lapping of waves.
I was on a pier with warehouse doors open to the
docks. Grey smoke surrounded me. I turned
toward the blue coyote in a trancelike state....*

Where were the rest of the entries? The last one was
dated April 22nd. It was now May 9th. Raven turned
page after page. All blank.

She was cold, achy and hungry. She felt light-
headed and walked over to the fridge, pulling on the
metal handle. The door didn't budge. She yanked
harder and the door made a loud *clunk* as it opened to
a half-eaten pizza, a container of milk and a shrivelled
apple. She picked up the bottle and removed the lid.
The smell of curdled milk made her nose wrinkle in
disgust. She quickly replaced the cap to stifle the
offensive odour.

She picked up the apple and carefully pared away
the wrinkled skin with a sharp knife. A few pieces were
still edible. At the table she pulled her wallet out of her
knapsack and counted her money. After purchasing the
bus ticket and buying something to eat on the ferry, she
had $172.53 left.

The footfall of heavy boots and a woman's shrill
laughter echoed up the stairs. Rita and Ted were

returning. Raven scooped up the money lying on the table and crammed it into her pocket just as the door flung open. Ted's hungry street eyes were quick to spot a secret. *What was she hiding in her hand?*

"You still here, kid? I thought you would have headed home by now," Ted sneered, slumping on one of the kitchen chairs. His eyes focused intently on Raven's pocket.

Rita hauled two battered suitcases from under her bed and flung them on the mattress. She marched over to Marcie's side of the room and started pulling clothes off the hangers and stuffing them into the suitcases.

"Aren't those my sister's clothes?" Raven protested.

"Yeah, I'm just taking back the stuff I lent her, that's all."

She grabbed an armful of tops and skirts, stuffed them into the suitcase and tried to force the lid shut.

"We're going to spend the night at our new place. Ted's found a great pad and besides, it'll give you some privacy. I know I told your dad I'd look after you, but Ted thinks we'd better be moving on and you seem to know what you're doing. I'll try to check in on you tomorrow, make sure you know your way around," she said, picking up one suitcase and walking down the hall to the stairs.

Ted got up slowly. His eyes remained fixed on Raven's pocket as he walked threateningly toward her.

A shrill voice screamed up the stairwell, "Ted, what the hell are you doing? Don't take all night. The cab is here!"

Ted reluctantly grabbed the other suitcase and scurried down the stairs to the waiting taxi.

The door swung closed with a loud *click*; Raven was alone in the city without Rita and only this dump for a roof over her head. She ran over and locked the door before again pulling the money out of her pocket. She laid it on the bed and split it into three piles. This way, if she were robbed, the thief wouldn't get all of it. Raven put some of the money in the front pocket of her backpack, some in her jeans' pocket and the rest in a handkerchief in her sock.

There wasn't much left in Marcie's closet. The empty wire hangers dangled from a wooden bar over-head. Raven grabbed an old sweater and a pair of faded jeans. Her sister would need a change of clothes when she found her. She stuffed the clothes and the diary into her knapsack, ready for tomorrow morning and her first day on the streets.

THREE

Marcie woke up after a three-day binge of booze, drugs and partying. Her head ached, her eyes were blurry. The chair she had passed out in was damp. She started to get up, but fell back into it. Her head throbbed. She tried to move slowly, to keep her body still. Some guy she didn't recognize lay passed out beside her. She raced for the bathroom and knelt in front of the toilet bowl. She knew she would be sick; she knew she *was* sick. When she pulled herself up off the filthy floor, each tiny movement caused her head to pound excruciatingly. She leaned over the sink and turned the tap on full blast, scooped cold water into her cupped palms and splashed it on her face and rinsed her mouth, wishing desperately for a toothbrush. She could swear her teeth were starting to rot.

She looked into the cracked mirror at a haggard

face, eyes dull and lifeless, hair tangled and matted. She ran her trembling fingers through the knots; the stranger in the mirror did the same.

"Oh god," she moaned. "Is this really me? Do I look this bad?"

She gently touched her cracked and swollen lips. Why were they so sore? What had she been doing for the past three days? Tripping on anything and everything she could get her hands on: first the whiskey and beer, then heroin, maybe even some coke. She couldn't remember who had passed her the first hit, but she wasn't picky. She would have gotten high with whoever happened to be around. She looked around the room now. Everyone was passed out; they would sleep until the next party started. They only awakened after dark, nocturnal animals slinking about the city streets.

How many of these people did she really *know* anyway? When it came down to it, they looked after themselves first. What did she care? It all seemed so long ago. So distant. Like her family. If they could see her now, they would be so ashamed. They might even feel *they* had failed *her* when it was so obviously the other way around. Some of the kids she'd met had left poor homes, others had left suburbia; some had run away from abusive parents, drunks, foster homes or Children's Aid, others were just bored and looking for attention. But she had left a *good* home....

Marcie half-stumbled, half-walked back to her apartment, her head hung to hide her embarrassing appearance. She said she'd quit drugs, said she was through with the parties, said when the next party rolled around she'd remember how sick she had been the morning after. This time she was determined to kick the habit.

It was 10 a.m. and her room was its usual mess. She looked around, realizing Rita had moved out. All of her clothes were gone except for a couple of faded tops and a pair of stained jeans. She snatched the clothes off the floor, reached for a bar of soap and a threadbare towel. In the drawer by the sink she looked for a pair of scissors and a comb. She walked down the hall to the washroom, turned the cold water tap on full blast and jumped into the tub, clothes and all. The water was freezing. Marcie leapt out of the tub, pulled the plug and stripped off her wet clothes. She had needed the shock to snap out of her stupor.

She ran a hot bath and waited while the tub filled. A new start needed a new image. Grabbing the scissors and a handful of her long, dark hair, she snipped off chunks that fell to the floor. She stuffed her shorn locks and old clothes into the garbage under the sink before getting into the tub, scrubbing her skin until it was sore, getting out and towelling off. After she dressed, she brushed her teeth again and went back to the room.

Marcie took a sip of juice, hoping she could keep it down. She hadn't had a good night's sleep in days. Her head was splitting, she was cold and her stomach was tied in a tight knot. She was in pain. She needed a fix. She began to sweat. She felt sick. Maybe she should just take a little something to get rid of the headache?

A rap on the door. Frightened, she lay quietly on the bed. Another rap on the door, then another.

"Go away! Just go away," she mumbled under her breath.

"Marcie? Marcie, are you in there?" a gentle voice questioned.

It was J.L. Thank god. She didn't want J.L. to see her like this, but she couldn't just leave him standing out there. She got up, opened the door and lurched back to the bed. She was in dire need of a hit, something to stabilize her. She managed to roll onto her back and fling her arm across her eyes.

"What's the matter?" J.L. asked, concerned.

"I was partying last night," Marcie mumbled. Her small body shivered on the bed.

J.L. grabbed a blanket and pulled it gently over her. "What happened to your beautiful hair?" he moaned.

"It will grow back, don't worry. I hurt all over. I've got to have something," she begged.

"That's why you're like this in the first place. You can't keep taking drugs. You've got to fight it." He sat on the edge of the bed holding her hand.

Marcie's body was stronger than her mind. It knew what it wanted, knew what it needed and knew what would make it feel good. She made it to the sink in time to retch. Shaking badly, she walked toward the closet, got the last shirt out of the cupboard, grabbed the towel and soap and headed for the door.

"I'll be right back," she mumbled.

J.L. sat at the kitchen table waiting while she

cleaned herself up. For the rest of the morning she
shook and threw up, but after several hours drifted off
to sleep. When she awoke she was pale, weak and
visibly shaken. She knew it was too soon to say she was
free of it all — she still yearned for that high, that
feeling of total bliss that lasted for only 20 seconds,
but tempted her every hour of every day.

◆

Raven sat in the restaurant in the bus depot eating
an egg sandwich. It had cost less than $2. She'd like
a hot chocolate, but it would cost another dollar.
She asked the woman at the counter for a cup of water
instead, then pulled her sister's diary out of her
knapsack and flipped through the pages looking for
the name of a street Marcie had mentioned in one of
the entries. It would be somewhere to start. She found
it: Hastings and a reference to a person named J.L.
After checking the free map of the city she had picked
up in the depot, she realized Hastings ran parallel to
the water. Raven folded the paper, stuffed it back into
her pocket and double-checked her directions with
the waitress.

"Hastings and where?"

"Hastings and Main," Raven replied, hopefully.

"Why do you want to go there? The strip is no place
for a young girl like you."

"I'm looking for my sister, Marcie," Raven confided.
She pulled out her wallet to show the woman Marcie's
picture.

Behind the picture, the waitress spotted a couple of $20s.

"Listen, kid. You're not going to get too far if you're this careless. You don't just flash your wallet around like that. Somebody spots those $20s and your wallet will be gone faster than you can blink. My advice to you is head home."

"I can't. I have to find her!"

"Well, if you're determined, then play it smart. Head out the main doors across to Main Street. Turn right, toward the north shore mountains. Main Street runs into Hastings. The corner of Main and Hastings is a dangerous place. Be prepared for anything. It isn't safe, even during the day."

"Thanks for your help," Raven said over her shoulder.

"Hold onto your bag and don't talk to anyone who looks suspicious," the waitress shouted after her.

Raven removed the picture of her sister from her wallet and placed it carefully inside her jacket pocket. In the same moment she spotted a man lying in the bushes. Should she get the police or an ambulance? Empty bottles of Pearl River Rice Wine were strewn on the ground. The man snorted and rolled over. He was alive, but barely.

She was too small to confront him herself, but she found it difficult to just walk away. Maybe someone inside the store on the corner would call for help? But when she told the shopkeeper, he just said it happened all the time and the guy would wake up eventually and stumble off.

She remembered learning about the effects of rice wine in D.A.R.E. class at her school. The visiting policeman had said it was more potent and dangerous than holding a revolver to your head; it killed brain cells that quickly. Not only that, he had warned, its high salt content would do permanent damage to your kidneys.

She continued walking to the intersection of Pender and Main: Chinatown. Bright red and yellow banners with Chinese writing painted on them hung in door-ways. Long bags of candy dangled from the awnings. Mandarin oranges strung on a silver wire stretched in the wind. Chinese music flowed from the open stores and upstairs windows. Storekeepers loudly advertised their wares to prospective buyers and patiently restacked the vegetables. Fish tanks full of live crabs, lobsters, oysters and conch shells stood next to aisles laden with plum sauce, green and red peppers and sugar cane. In a restaurant window a glazed duck on a rotisserie turned slowly in a barbecue steam.

Despite the tempting sights and smells, she stuck to her mission and kept walking. At the corner of Main and Hastings, she turned left and walked along the north side of the street. A small group of men hung around the alleyway by a hotel. A sign in a window said: NO DRUGS. NO DEALING. NO LOITERING. YOU ARE BEING VIDEO TAPED. One man's jerky body movements reminded her of Ted last night when he had said he "needed a fix." He was obviously ill, mentally and physically. She quickly averted her eyes and walked on. Just past the hotel, a man hovered over a heating vent for warmth. His fingers were dark red and looked like large sausages. His other hand was swollen and looked broken. He slouched down and his head slumped forward on his chest as he leaned back against a wall. Dried blood caked the front of his shirt. Raven knew that these people, like the man passed out on rice wine, were "regulars" and that the store and hotel owners wouldn't bother calling the ambulance unless it was a matter of life and death.

Farther down the block a woman lay passed out in a doorway. A man sat nearby, guarding her. His back rested against the wall. There was no telling how long he had been waiting for her to come to. A hotel at the end of the block was playing loud honky-tonk music. The smell of stale beer and the sound of drunken laughter floated out of its swinging doors. Raven passed a pawnshop. The sign out front read: TOP CASH PAID. People streamed in and out carrying radios, televisions and CDs. At the next corner a small triangular park was home to people passed out on benches. One woman, talking loudly, stopped long enough to grab a brown sack from the guy next to her. She tilted the bag toward her mouth and took a long swig.

Raven passed clothing stores with metal bars on the windows and farther along there was a well-stocked meat market with two pink neon pigs above the store's entrance way. Most of the other buildings along the street were boarded up. Printed in bold letters across the next building were the words: VANCOUVER SECURITY K-9 PATROL. At the next corner Raven paused by a concrete monument with wreaths placed at its base.

She skirted around the monument and walked up the pathway to a park bench to rest her weary feet. Everyone in the park recognized a "green kid" when they saw one. She didn't belong here. She was no street person — too squeaky clean. She looked for someone with a friendly face to turn to. An old woman with a shopping cart wheeled past. Raven approached her, taking the picture out of her pocket.

"Excuse me," Raven inquired, holding out the photo.

The old woman, blind in one eye and hard of hearing, hadn't seen Raven. As soon as she focused, she started screaming at the top of her lungs. "Leave me alone! They're coming! Now, see what you've done? Got a hide…run…you've made them mad," wailed the old woman as she shook her gloved fist in the air.

Raven backed away slowly. The old woman pulled her tattered coat tightly around her, turned abruptly and walked away, cursing.

"Whatcha want girlie?" a small, fat woman on a park bench called out.

"My, my sis…sister's lost. I'm trying to find her," stuttered Raven.

"You got a picture or something?" the old woman interrupted.

Raven approached her carefully, still shaken from her last encounter.

"Well, do you want to find your sister or not? I ain't got all day," snapped the stranger.

"I'm sorry, " Raven choked, handing her the picture.

She looked at it, then at Raven. "I haven't seen her lately," the woman replied.

"Then you know her?" Raven said excitedly.

"Nope. Didn't say I knew her. Just seen her around that's all."

"When did you see her last?" Raven insisted.

"Can't remember. Days, months, hours — they're all the same down here. Makes no difference, no difference. Besides, I haven't seen her at this end of the strip. That one hangs out by death's door anyhow," the woman whispered.

"Where is that?"

"You watch yourself, girlie. Remember what old Bertie is telling you."

"Do you know a J.L.?" Raven asked.

"Nope," the old woman said abruptly, getting up.

Raven started to walk down the hill.

The old woman yelled after her, "What's your name, kid? If I hear anything, I'll let you know. I'm always in the park this time of day."

"Raven," she answered, waving goodbye to the old woman.

Raven headed back down the strip on the south side of Hastings Street. A gang of men who looked South American milled about at the next corner. One of the men was flashing hand signals, gestures that must have meant something to someone else "reading" them across the street. A dark blue van stopped and two of the men walked over. One passed the driver a small packet. The man walked back to the group counting money. A woman loped along behind him, her arms dangling as she reached out to him. He zigzagged, trying to lose her. Her long, skinny arms swung in front of her like a monkey's. The man threw a small piece of paper on the ground and she pounced on it, but it was empty — he had tricked her. She slumped in a doorway, exhausted.

Raven quickly averted her face in an attempt to avoid staring. A man stepped directly in her path and blocked her way. Terrified, she sidestepped him and hurried across the intersection.

She stopped at a small grocery store, purchased two apples, a box of animal crackers and a bottle of pop. Her feet hurt from all her walking. Outside the store, three teenaged boys were hanging around on roller blades. One wore only a trench coat and shorts and was covered in tattoos. He passed a small packet to the two younger guys, then skated away.

Raven munched nervously on her animal crackers and watched the people across the street in Pigeon Park. A man lay on the ground, passed out cold, with his eye swollen shut. His hair was encrusted with dried blood. She crossed the street then carefully skirted around him as she walked cautiously toward another group of men huddled on a bench.

"I'm trying to find my sister," Raven pleaded. Her small hands trembled as she held out the picture.

"Beat it, kid," snarled one of the men.

Raven turned away. She showed the picture to

everyone in the park, but it was always the same answer: "Nope, haven't seen her."

She looked for a telephone to call Rita. Maybe she had returned. The hall phone at the hotel rang and rang; she expected she'd be on her own again tonight. It was too late to phone her father at the store. She'd have to wait until tomorrow to leave him a message.

Earlier a policeman on patrol had warned her of a demented woman wandering the streets sticking people with an infected needle. As a result Raven constantly looked over her shoulder, afraid the woman would sneak up on her and stab her when her back was turned.

It was late afternoon and she was weary and a bit lost. She looked down alleys for an empty fire escape to safely perch on while she looked at her map. She found an accessible ladder and climbed two flights to the top. She made herself comfortable, propping her knapsack under her head for a pillow, and took the map from her pocket. Suddenly, she heard voices below her. She would be undetected as long as she didn't make any sudden noises or movements. Raven inched up over the stair so that she could see the people below, but made sure to remain out of their line of vision.

"Can I interest you in doing a little Chui Lung ladies?" a man chuckled. He reached into his pocket and pulled out tin foil and a straw.

"Yeah, light it up, man," a girl said eagerly.

The man held a lighter under the foil as the two young girls took turns chasing the dragon's tail of curling smoke.

The noxious fumes rose upward to Raven. Afraid she would sneeze, she stuck her index finger under her nose, but a tiny, muffled *achooo* escaped.

"Did you hear something?" one girl mumbled.

"Nah, it's just the wind. Time to get back to work. You've only been out there for six hours — half a day, yet you still haven't earned your keep. See you back here in a couple of hours and be sure to make it worth my while," the man ordered. The trio split up, the girls going in one direction, the man in the other.

Raven huddled on the fire escape until she was sure they were not coming back. A cold wind had picked up, chilling her through and through. It carried the scent of the urine-drenched alley up to her nostrils. She grabbed her knapsack and walked along Jackson Street — according to the map, this was the way to Oppenheimer Park, a place her sister had mentioned in her diary.

Raven walked until she came to a sign that indicated she was in the right place. She sat on a bench and watched people coming and going. No one appeared to have anywhere to go. Raven decided to survey the passersby about her sister. She showed the picture to an elderly woman, who passed it to an old man seated beside her.

"Ralph, you remember this girl?" the woman said loudly.

"Yeah, she was working for some Lonnie guy last I heard," he said, nodding his head. "If you don't want to end up dead, stay far away from him. You'll find him and his junkies hanging around the Balmoral Hotel most nights," he wheezed.

"Where is the Balmoral?"

"Close to death's door, the gateway, the entrance into the pit," he coughed.

"How can I find it?"

"You don't find it. It finds you. Some are foolish enough to hang around shooting up, others take the easy way out — commit suicide. They skydive off the roof of the hotel."

The old woman told the man to leave Raven alone; he was just scaring her.

Raven headed out of the park past a man who was passed out with his head propped against a tree trunk. As she neared him, an unpleasant odour floated toward her and she saw he was covered in open sores. He obviously needed more help than she could offer. She felt helpless on these streets. How could they survive out here? Who *did* take care of them?

FOUR

Twilight descended like a grey cloak over the city. It was Raven's first night on the streets. What her mother would have called "unsavoury characters" prowled the garbage-strewn alleyways; they were drawn magnetically to the corner of Main and Hastings.

She walked until she came to a group of teenagers hanging out in front of the Balmoral Hotel. She didn't know if Lonnie was one of them, but she walked up to one of the girls in the group to inquire.

"Is Lonnie here?" Raven asked tentatively.

"What's it to you?" the girl scoffed.

"I'm trying to find my sister." She held out the picture.

"Where'd you get that?" the girl demanded.

"It's my sister. Do you know her?" Raven asked hopefully.

"What's it to you if I do or don't?" the girl challenged.

She gave Raven a hard push on the shoulder.

"Please, I've got to find her. Bertie told me she was down in this area," Raven pleaded.

"Well, you ain't gonna find her here. Old Bertie should mind her own damn business," the girl snapped, grabbing the picture out of Raven's hand, scrunching it up and tossing it on the ground.

Raven picked it up, smoothed it out and walked down the block.

"Do you know Bertie?" someone whispered from the shadows.

"Yes, I know her. What's it to you?" Raven snapped, shocking herself.

"*Shh!* Keep your voice down. Start walking and don't look back," he said.

"Why should I? Who are you?" Raven asked.

"I'm a friend of Bertie's. Maybe I can help you. Let me see the picture."

Raven pulled the crumpled photo out of her pocket and passed it to him. He looked at it and then passed it back.

"Well, do you know her or not?" Raven asked.

"Stay quiet and keep on walking. Yeah, I know her," he warned. He quickened his pace. Raven had to hurry to keep up with him. He turned the corner onto Main Street and stopped. "Why the hell are you asking those guys where she is? Are you looking to get iced or something?"

"What do you mean?" Raven gulped.

"They're pushers, drug dealers. They work for Lonnie.

If anyone messes with him or talks to the cops, they're history. A snitch's life is less than worthless on these streets. No witnesses, no testimonies — that's the rule. Your sister used to hang out with their boss. When she found out what a low life he was, she probably took off."

"Then they know where she is. I'm going back there to make them tell me," Raven stormed.

"The hell you aren't. Weren't you listening? Those people would just as soon kill you as look at you. You don't even know who you're messing with! The word on the street is she's probably dead anyway. Nobody's seen or heard from her in days."

"I don't believe that. I'm going to get some food, go back to the room and track her down," Raven replied.

"Well, if you're going to last a minute on the streets, you'd better learn the ropes," he said.

As they walked past storefront vendors still open for night business, her new friend slipped fruit into his pockets.

"What are you doing? You can't steal that," Raven protested loudly.

"*Shh!* Keep your voice down," he whispered.

Raven followed him, but as soon as they rounded the corner he stopped.

"If you don't steal down here, you don't eat. Got it? The minimum I can survive on is $5 a day and I barely make that panhandling. I have to shoplift when I'm desperate. That's life, mine anyway. Hey, *you* got any money?" he asked.

"A little," Raven hedged.

"Can you buy some milk for our supper?" he asked.

"OK, I guess so. Just don't steal anything else." She went into the store to buy a carton of milk and two candy bars.

He grinned sheepishly at her and said, "Let's go," as they headed southeast toward an industrial area.

"Where are we going? Is this the way to Marcie's apartment?" Raven asked.

"There's someone I want you to meet first; then I'll walk you back to her place," he replied. "By the way, I'm Ben."

They continued on in silence. After a few minutes, Ben stopped in front of a deserted warehouse door locked with a heavy padlock. He walked over to the corner of the building, stooped over and grasped a corrugated metal panel. He held the bottom corner away and motioned for Raven to go in, replacing the wall panel with practised precision. Raven tried to look around the barely lit interior of the building, but the feeble light made it hard for her eyes to adjust. Ben ushered her into a small back room.

"There's no place like home," he said.

Raven heard someone talking; they weren't alone. On the far side of the room, an old woman, slightly familiar, sat reciting a story to two young children.

"I'm home," Ben called.

"You're late, Ben. Anna and Robert were starting to worry about you," the old woman said with concern in her voice.

"I got sidetracked. Sorry," he said.

"Well, never mind. You're home safe now. Who is this with you, then?"

"Her name's Raven," he replied.

"I remember you from the park. You were searching for your sister, right? My eyes aren't so good anymore. Broke my glasses a few years back," Bertie said. Raven stepped closer so the woman could see her more clearly. "You must be tired. Sit down and rest a while."

"Time for supper. Okay, everybody ante up. What you got?" Ben prodded. He pulled the stolen fruit from his pocket and placed it on the old packing crate that doubled as a table.

Bertie pulled some day-old buns out of her bag. "Pretty slim pickings. You got anything, kids?" Anna produced a half-eaten hot dog she had found in the park. Robert held back, not wanting to share his find with Raven.

"Come on. Do you have something or not?" Ben persisted.

"Do we gotta share with her?" the boy whined as he jerked his head in Raven's direction. He was about eight, her brother's age.

"You know the rules. Everybody at the table eats, whether they brought something or not."

Robert reluctantly pulled two boxes of cold, greasy fries out of his pocket. He placed both on the crate.

"Have you been dumpster diving again? You know I told you to stay out of those bins," Ben said authoritatively.

"No, I found these on the tables outside," he protested.

Ben sliced the apples and orange into equal pieces. There were five buns, enough for everyone to have one. Ben cut the hot dog in half. He gave half to Anna and half to Robert. Bertie divided the fries equally between them.

"You've got some milk, right Raven?" Ben reminded her.

Raven reached into her backpack and pulled out the carton of milk. He poured half of the milk into Bertie's special china bowl, old and cracked, but rimmed with delicate roses, then placed Bertie's bun in the milk to soak. Her teeth weren't as good as they used to be. It was an especially good night if they had milk. Most nights Bertie had to soak her stale bun in water.

"Wait a minute. I have a couple of chocolate bars," Raven announced.

The children's eyes widened in anticipation. "Can we eat the chocolate first?" they chimed in chorus.

"Well, I don't know. What do you think Bertie?" Ben hedged.

"Won't hurt them none. Long as they eat the rest of their supper," Bertie chuckled softly. "Cut the bars in four."

"Don't you want a little, Bertie?" Ben asked her. He knew how much she loved chocolate.

"You children will eat my share, won't you?" she coaxed.

The children grinned. Ben split the bars into four equal pieces.

Ben was worried about Bertie; she tired so easily lately and had trouble sleeping. Her breathing was becoming more and more laboured. Quite often she had pain in her chest that lasted for long periods. He tried to convince her to go to the free medical clinic with him, but she wouldn't admit she was ill.

After dinner, the children begged for a story. "Tell us about when you were a dancer, Bertie."

"Well, that was a long time ago. Yes, indeed, a long, long time ago. I was barely 16 at the time. A travelling road show came to town with women in beautiful costumes and actors decked out in fancy attire. I attended every performance. I couldn't get enough of the excitement, the laughter. When the show left town, I begged them to take me with them. They hired me on as an assistant and I filled in when one of the girls got sick. The show travelled from one town to another, but eventually it folded and I found myself alone in Vancouver, a strange city. I was far away from my hometown with nothing to return to. My folks had moved away while I was on the road. I tried to find a job in the city, but work was scarce. Finally, I found a job as an understudy in a play — when the leading lady got sick, I got my lucky break. The day after the debut, the reviews in the paper mentioned me by name, even said I might have a starring role of my own one day," Bertie reminisced fondly.

"Tell us about your costume, Bertie," the children prompted.

"My costume? Yes, my costume. Well, the gown was a midnight-blue crushed velvet. I wore my long hair scooped up in a net with diamond-studded facets. The stage lights reflected their glimmering shine when I danced and I actually was *brilliant*. I was special, really special." Her eyes misted over. "At least I have the memory. I'll always have that," she whispered. "Well, enough of all this nonsense. Time for bed, you two. It's after your bedtime already. You don't want Bertie to get cross, do you?" she said.

Ben grinned; he had never heard Bertie utter an unkind word since he had known her. The children obediently got ready for bed, climbing into old sleeping bags, ragged and worn out, but clean.

Bertie sat down on the edge of an old mattress and began singing softly to the children, "She wheels her wheelbarrow through streets broad and narrow, crying cockles and mussels, alive, alive-o."

◆

An hour later, Ben had escorted Raven back to her room and had whistled happily all the way back to the warehouse.

"Bertie, I'm back," he whispered as he entered their squatter's hideaway.

"Did you see Raven safely to her door?" Bertie asked.

"Yes. I told her I'd meet her at noon tomorrow and help her look for her sister," Ben replied.

"Did you remember to ask her to the surprise party tomorrow night?"

"Yes," Ben said.

"Well, you can help me finish the decorations, then," said Bertie.

They made party hats out of folded newspaper. Bertie had been saving scrap material for weeks to make the birthday festive. She had fashioned origami birds, flowers and garlands out of pieces of tin foil, paper and coloured plastic.

"Tomorrow I'll take the little ones over to Mrs. Larson's for the day. When we leave, can you decorate the room to surprise the children?" Bertie asked.

"Sure. I'll do it just the way you showed me," Ben promised.

"Do you have enough for Robert's harmonica?" Bertie asked.

"Yes, but I'm short $5 for the cake. I should be able to panhandle enough for that."

"Here, I've got enough for the book. I'll spot you $5. I can easily earn it tomorrow. If you make a couple of dollars panhandling, be sure to buy candles and a sparkler."

Ben grinned and nodded. Ever since Anna and Robert's family had died in a fire and Bertie had taken them in, she had wanted to celebrate the children's birthdays. Because Anna and Robert didn't know the true dates, Bertie had picked a day at random and celebrated both together.

◆

Marcie awoke to the sound of the door closing behind J.L. She had stayed at his apartment last night, afraid that Lonnie would come looking for her at her own place. She had slept on the couch and had a bad kink in her neck. She got up and stretched, walked over to the fridge and took out a carton of orange juice.

Yesterday, after passing out and waking to an empty apartment, she had been startled by a harsh rap on the door; Lonnie had slammed his fist into it like a battering ram, so hard that it had ricocheted off the wall.

"Where the hell have you been? I ain't seen or heard from you in days," he had accused, towering over her.

Marcie had taken a few steps backward, but he had grabbed her roughly by the arm and jerked her toward him.

"Answer me, damn it. Where have you been?" he had snarled.

"I was here the whole time. I was sick."

"You got somebody else or something?" His vise-like grip had intensified, threatening to snap her arms like twigs.

"No, there's no one else," Marcie had gasped, afraid to tell him that they were through.

"There'd better not be, or I'll have to kill him," he had promised coldly. His tight hold had relaxed on her arm. Telltale red finger welts, discoloured her skin.

"Get ready. We're going to party," he had ordered.

"I don't want to go to any more parties," Marcie had said quietly.

"Why not?" Lonnie had snapped.

"Because I'm through with drugs."

"Yeah, sure. Me too," Lonnie had chuckled.

"No. I'm serious."

"Yeah, well we'll see. You'll be crawling out of your skin without a fix. You know where to find me when you need me. It won't take long before you come begging for a little picker-upper. Suit yourself. There'll be plenty of other girls at the party anyway," Lonnie had yelled over his shoulder.

Marcie had stood at the door listening to his heavy feet tromping down the stairwell.

Lonnie often hit the girls who worked for him. They learned to do whatever he said and fast. There was no telling when he'd fly into a violent rage. When Marcie first started going out with Lonnie, he couldn't do enough to convince her it was all worth it. His main girl, Jilly, was soon forgotten. He was too busy grooming Marcie to bother with Jilly anymore.

Jilly still hung around, hoping Lonnie would get tired of Marcie and take her back. She disappeared for hours each day, but always returned with money. Once, when he thought she'd kept some for herself, he smacked her hard across the mouth and told her she hadn't been earning her keep.

When he finished berating Jilly, he realized that Marcie had seen the whole sordid episode and he turned on his false charm. She fell for it, and soon she found herself in Jilly's position...Lonnie's property. She would be his to do with as he wanted. Once he had someone in his clutches, it was impossible to break free. He told her she owed the group, would have to start working and contributing her share.

◆

"I'm going to do what I came to do. Get a job," Marcie told J.L. later in the park. "I'm through with Lonnie, with every part of that life. I've learned my lesson," she pledged.

"He's very dangerous, you know. His brother is the centre of the drug trade. Whatever goes in or out of the harbour, his brother has a hand in. Lonnie is his right-hand man. He pushes drugs. He also supplies him with young runaways," J.L. told her.

"What do you mean 'supplies him with young runaways'?"

"The word on the street is that the same ship that brings in the drugs takes a return cargo of young kids to various ports in Asia," said J.L.

"Lonnie always went out of his way to talk to young kids, looked out for them on the streets. When they arrived with nowhere to turn, or no money, he was the first to buy them food or give them spending money or new clothes. He even helped send some of them home," Marcie said.

"What do you mean 'send them home'?" J.L. asked.

"Well, he got Jake to take them to the bus depot

and gave Jake money to buy them a ticket home."

"Did you ever see or hear from any of them again?"

"No."

"You mean *everyone* he talked to decided to go back to the small towns or suburbs or wherever they were running away from?" J.L. challenged. "Don't you find that a bit suspicious? Jake probably drove them to the docks."

"Lonnie did make a mark in his book every time he sent a new kid home. I asked him about it and he chuckled and said he was just keeping track of his good deeds. I didn't think anything of it at the time."

A record of the names. Perhaps his sister's name was in that book, J.L. thought. He had promised his mother he would find her, but when he had shown her picture on the streets everyone who remembered seeing her said she had only been around for a day or two — they hadn't seen her again after that.

"Do you know where he keeps his book?" J.L. said guardedly.

"Yes. In his safe. Just before Jilly disappeared, she told me she was tired of Lonnie beating her up all the time. She said she had jacked his duplicate set and they contained enough evidence to put him behind bars for a long time. She said she didn't want to end up like some of his other girls — missing, dead or sold. I didn't believe her. I thought she was just jealous," Marcie admitted.

"Did she tell you where she stashed it?"

"In her room. She lived in the same room I live in

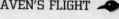

now. She was roommates with Rita before I moved in. She didn't tell me where in the room she had hidden it, but it shouldn't be too hard to find. The next thing I knew, she was missing."

FIVE

Raven woke up the next morning in Marcie's room and decided to get an early start. She and Ben had discussed places to search for her sister last night while he had walked her home. First, she needed to find a telephone. The one in the hall said: OUT OF ORDER. She decided to walk back to the bus depot to use the pay phones there. The ones on the streets around here were broken or too risky — standing around was an open invitation to get robbed, harassed or even stabbed with a stray needle. Most of the people down here were too stoned or mentally ill to even know what they were doing.

When she got to the depot, she dialled the operator and asked for assistance placing a long-distance call.

"Just tell me the number," the operator said kindly.

"I don't know the number, but I can tell you the

name of the store and the store owner's name," Raven replied.

"That's fine. I'll look it up," the operator offered. A few seconds passed and then she said, "I have the store on the line. How do you wish to pay for the call?"

"Collect," she said nervously.

"What was that? I'm afraid you'll have to speak up. I can't hear you," the operator instructed.

"I want to call collect please. Please say 'It's Raven. Jim's girl,'" Raven answered.

Frank answered and said, "Hello? Raven, is that you? How are you?"

"I'm fine, but I haven't found Marcie yet and my cousin Rita is mixed up in something and never around. Can you please give my father that message and ask him to tell me what he thinks I should do? I'll phone back tomorrow."

"Are you all right? Are you in any danger?"

"No, I'm safe, but I need advice. I have a few leads and someone who knows the area, but I need to know what Mom and Dad think I should do."

"I'll take the message over later today, as soon as I close the store."

◆

Even though it was early in the morning, people hung around the washrooms in front of the Carnegie Centre. Raven searched every face, hoping to see her sister's. Absent-mindedly, she reached into her pocket and pulled out the necklace Marcie had given to her for her last birthday. She gazed fondly at the raven medallion and put it around her neck; she was determinaed to find her sister. She prayed Marcie was safe and that she could soon put her parents at ease.

She continued along the street as the dealers called out to her as she walked by.

"What you want? Up? Down?"

A guy walked by and muttered under his breath, "How much?"

The dealer closest to him responded, "Coke, $20. Heroin, $10."

A dark green van pulled into the alley adjacent to the centre. The sign on the van read: DEYAS NEEDLE EXCHANGE. Three young guys with squeegees stood on the street corner looking for car windows to wash. As soon as they saw the van pull in, they scurried over to it like crabs after a choice bit of meat. They made the trade and then retreated into the alley.

Their arms were reduced to pincushions, littered with track marks from shooting up. A tag read: LOST ALLEY — A SHOOTING GALLERY FOR THE WALKING DEAD. Raven thought that whoever had spray-painted that on the alley wall knew what they were talking about. A small green fern clung to one of the jagged cracks in the alley wall. She felt a sudden wave of home-sickness as she remembered the lush green of the salal in the woods near the campground.

Raven walked past a woman picking things up off the ground, but on closer inspection she realized the woman was obviously hallucinating, imagining that she was picking up crumbs of crack and putting them in her lap. She cocked her head to one side, listening. Raven saw the crazed look in the woman's eyes and backed away. The muscles around her mouth twitched. In the next doorway a girl no more than 14 or 15 lay in a comalike sleep, open sores around her mouth and a length of glass tubing poking out of her pocket. Her hair was matted, her coat torn and filthy. Her fingertips were caked with thick black dirt.

◆

Raven returned to Oppenheimer Park, convinced that someone there might be able to give her a lead. Besides, she and Ben had arranged to meet there before conducting another search. It was a high-traffic area and the odds were better.

A man in his late 50s was acting very oddly; his antics had more in common with a child than someone of his age. He tiptoed behind two men and a woman. Every time they stopped, the man ran and hid behind a tree. Two other men sat close by, watching.

"Bushy Tail, Bushy Tail," they shouted in chorus, pointing at the squirrel-like man and laughing.

"I don't have a bushy tail," he shouted back.

"Bushy Tail, Bushy Tail," the men boomed.

"I don't have a bushy tail. You do!" he taunted. Indignantly, he looked over his shoulder to see if he *had* sprouted a tail. Satisfied he hadn't, he scampered merrily down the street.

Raven found a rickety chair and watched as a very

young woman with a stroller and a small boy in tow entered the park. She sat down beside Raven while her little boy raced over to a park attendant to ask for a tricycle. When the park employee went inside the long shack and came out carrying one, the boy's face lit up in delight and he climbed on and pedalled back and forth in front of the building.

Close to the building, Raven spotted syringe caps, discarded needles, wrappers, spitball bags, condoms and beer bottles in danger of being stepped on or picked up by curious toddlers. How many of these children would grow up to live on the street, use needles or heroin like the girls she had seen in the alley?

The young mother struck up a conversation, saying that she was terrified to live here. She barricaded her door each night against thieves in search of items to steal and pawn for drug money. She tried to sleep between seven and midnight, then stay awake to guard against intruders. She heard rats scurrying about in the dark, chewing on the corner of her mattress, the food in the cupboards, even the plastic lid of her deodorant bottle. She told Raven she had finally saved enough money from her meagre welfare cheque to buy chicken wire to surround the baby's crib.

A group of people on the west side of the park congregated in front of All Tribes Mission. A rag-tag line started to assemble as the deep sound of a whistle marked the noon hour. Men and women exited the building, devouring bologna and peanut butter sandwiches. An old woman in an electric wheelchair zoomed past Raven, stopping here and there to ask, "When are the videos going to start?" No one seemed to know, so she zipped down to the other end of the building to look for the park attendant.

"Hi, Raven. Sorry I'm late," Ben apologized, walking up to her.

"That's OK, I'm enjoying the sunshine," Raven answered.

"Did you have any luck this morning?" Ben asked.

Raven shook her head sadly.

"I have to pick up a few things for the party and be back to the warehouse by five o'clock."

"How did you all end up living in a warehouse anyway? Why doesn't Bertie have a proper place to live?" Raven asked.

"She used to, but she's scared to live there now. She lived in a housekeeping room on the downtown east side. One day, a young guy started hanging around her building. He seemed friendly, but turned out to be a professional. He gained the confidence of the elderly tenants by being kind to them and managed to get into the building. Then he started taking advantage and moved in with Bertie's neighbour, George. George didn't even protest at first, but this guy took over, slept in George's bed, didn't pay any rent and ate his food. He didn't give him a cent. If George protested, he beat him up. George was too scared to go to the police, afraid he would really get it if he ratted on him. He roughed him up regularly anyway.

"George kept a running bar tab at the Dodson Hotel.

He'd cash his cheque at the hotel and pay his beer tab, then he paid his rent and bought a few groceries, but whatever was left over from his pension cheque was confiscated. When George's friends went in with baseball bats, the bully got the message and took off, but a few months later George turned up dead. Bertie was scared and decided to move out. She said she'd rather live on the streets. Anyway, that's the story."

"People think that everyone who lives down here is depraved or wasted, but there must be dozens of stories like Bertie's, like yours," Raven said.

"You'll notice a lot of regulars as we walk up the strip. If I see any I know, I'll ask them if they've seen your sister lately."

They walked south through the intersection of Main and Hastings. Raven was amazed at the crowd congregated in front of the Carnegie Centre. Earlier in the morning there had been only a smattering of people, but now the stairs were jam-packed. A dozen or so folding tables displaying all sorts of wares made it look almost like a bazaar.

"Come on, let's get going. Look, there's Gertrude up ahead."

"Hi, Gertrude. May I carry your bags?" Ben asked when they had reached her.

"Ben. It's good to see you. Yes, I could use a hand. How's Bertie doing these days?"

"Not too well. She's been having a few more spells lately. I'm worried about her."

"She's a tough one, old Bertie. She knows enough

to go to the doctor when she has to. Don't you worry."

"Gertrude, this is Raven. She's a friend of mine."

"Raven. That's a very beautiful name."

"My grandmother named me. It's nice to meet you, Gertrude," Raven replied.

"Well, shall we go to my place? I haven't had guests in a long time. No, indeed, not in a very long time."

Ben and Raven each carried a bag. They turned the corner heading east on Keefer Street.

"We have to go around back. The bolt on the front fence is broken." She led them around the house and through the alley. The yard was strewn with debris: an old washing machine, a mattress and a car up on blocks. "Watch your step here, the sidewalk is cracked."

Broken glass and rusted cans littered the walkway. Raven wondered if Gertrude lived in this huge old house by herself. They walked up three flights of stairs to the top landing. Gertrude was extremely winded. She grasped the railing for support, saying her back "hurt something fierce." She took a deep breath, then rummaged around in her purse for her key.

"That's strange. I could have sworn I put it in my purse. Perhaps it's under the mat. Can you check, Ben?"

Ben put the bag down and searched under the mat. "No. Nothing here."

"Oh, my! I'm getting so forgetful. Now what did I do with the darn thing? Think, think. Yes, I remember — my pocket." She slipped her hand inside her pocket and retrieved the key. "Here it is. Thank goodness."

The old door creaked loudly as it swung open. Ben

and Raven followed her into the small bed-sitting room. Gertrude bustled about putting her things away. She untied her hat and hung it up on a nail protruding from the wall.

"Sit down, sit down. I'll put us on a pot of tea." She filled an old pot with water, placed it on the hot plate and turned it on high.

Raven and Ben both looked around for a place to sit. Ben perched on the windowsill and motioned for Raven to sit down on the foot of the bed.

"Do you like your tea strong or weak?"

"Weak, thanks," they both replied.

"Because if you like it strong, I can always use a new tea bag." Gertrude grabbed an old tea bag off the towel rack and popped it into the boiling water. "I can get two pots of tea from one bag if I'm careful."

She plopped herself down into the small wooden rocking chair. "Now, then, we'll let the tea steep a mite. Tell me about yourself, Raven. What brings you to the city?"

"I'm looking for my sister, Marcie." Raven held out the picture, wondering how Gertrude knew she wasn't *from* the city.

"She's a pretty girl, just like you."

"Have you seen her around?" Ben asked.

"Seen her around? Oh my, no!" she replied absent-mindedly.

Raven was curious about how Gertrude ended up living in a place like this. She didn't seem to fit. Her speech and manner showed signs of a good upbringing.

Ben poured the tea and handed one mug to Gertrude and one to Raven.

On the small nightstand next to Gertrude's bed was a silver picture frame. It held a photo of a very distinguished-looking man. Lying next to the frame was a brush and mirror set with silver inlaid handles. On the back of the mirror, the single silver initial *G* was written in fancy script. The three expensive-looking pieces were totally out of place. Raven looked around the room: everything else was either makeshift or shoddy.

"Did you always live here, Gertrude?"

Gertrude thought for a few seconds. "Did I always live here? Why, no…I used to live in West Vancouver, but that was a long time ago."

"When did you move?"

"Years ago, after I started work as a waitress. It wasn't always this way. I used to live in a proper house, a splendid house. My husband, Mr. Dodson, was a busy lawyer, you know. He had a booming practice. We often entertained his clients."

"What did you do, Gertrude?"

"Do? Why, look after Mr. Dodson, of course."

"What do you mean?"

"Well, every morning I got Mr. Dodson ready for work. I took pride in making sure his shirt, tie and coat matched. I laid them out in a row on the bed. I know he appreciated it. Why, he even told me so once… besides it certainly kept my days quite full, quite full."

"Did you ever have another kind of job, outside the

house?" Raven asked. She couldn't believe Gertrude hadn't had to lift a finger in those days. Her own mother worked from dawn until well after Raven and her brothers were in bed doing household chores.

"Me? Why, no. I was much too busy. I had to plan the menu with the cook each day and, of course, if we were entertaining, it was doubly difficult. Mr. Dodson liked things just so. Yes, indeed. It was my job to supervise the housekeeper, make sure all the flowers were fresh."

Raven recalled Tim and Allan picking handfuls of wildflowers and jamming them into old jars to surprise their mom. She and Gertrude were worlds apart.

"Where was I? Oh my. Yes, I was telling you about… Mr. Dodson. He was quite adamant that everything be spit and polish. The silverware had to shine until you could see your face in it. The chandelier had to be cleaned one crystal at a time. And believe you me, if the housekeeper missed one, Mr. Dodson would be sure to detect it. Certainly, it was a full-time job *being* Mrs. Dodson. At least it used to be. Then one day my whole world fell apart. The police came to the door and told me he had been killed in a car crash."

"What did you do? Did you have any family nearby?"

"No. I'm an only child, as was my husband; both sets of parents had long ago passed on. Mr. Dodson had mortgaged the house heavily. I had never done any other kind of work. I soon found out there weren't many openings for hostesses. The only jobs I could find paid minimum wage. I had no hope of keeping up the mortgage payments on our home with that income. My only alternative was to move out."

"What about insurance?"

"My husband had let the policy lapse. I was on my own — no skills and few prospects. In fact, I had *never* held down a job. I got married right after high school."

"What did you do?"

"I got a job waiting tables. My wages didn't pay for rent on a big place as well as groceries, so a waitress I worked with told me about these housekeeping rooms. I checked them out and decided to move in."

"How long have you lived in this neighbourhood?"

"Too long, child. Too long. And now I'm retired. I'll never be able to move out with my small pension cheque. I have enough, though…enough to pay my rent and just feed myself."

She sat quietly for a few moments, then drifted off into a light sleep. Raven looked at Ben, concerned. He shrugged his shoulders and grinned. They sat still, not wanting to disturb Gertrude, but unsure whether they should stay or leave. Gertrude shifted slightly in the rocker and sat up straight, blinking.

"Oh, hello Ben. When did you get here? And who's this with you, then?"

Ben played along, pretending they had just arrived. He winked at Raven. "We just got here. We thought we'd drop by and say hello."

"That's nice," she smiled and drifted back to sleep.

Ben signalled that it was time to go. The door shut quietly behind them.

"Is she all right, Ben?"

"Yeah, she's drifted off like that for as long as I can remember. I think it's her way of escaping. Gertrude might not have any control over where she lives, but she has control over how much time she spends awake, experiencing it. We'd better head back downtown to get the present and the cake. It's almost time."

"What are you getting Robert?"

"A harmonica. He's wanted one for so long. He's so musical, it seems a shame he doesn't have an instrument. Bertie is looking after the present for Anna."

SIX

Earlier that morning, Bertie had dropped off the children at Mrs. Larson's, humming softly to herself as she had continued on to the store where she had bought two dozen pencils at $2 a pack. She had walked to the corner of Hastings and Abbott and raked around in her knapsack for her faithful old tin cup, then had popped the pencils into it — she was open for business.

"Pencils for sale!" Bertie had called out as people passed by.

"How much are the pencils?" a girl had asked.

"It's by donation," Bertie had replied.

The girl had put a toonie in the cup and taken two pencils.

"Thank you, have a good day," Bertie had said. Her feet had ached. She had dearly wanted a cup of tea, but hadn't dared use any of the money. By lunchtime she had sold 10 more pencils at 50¢ each. She was still $2 short if she wanted to get the special pop-up book for Anna.

Now Bertie unscrewed the lid of her water jar and took a long drink. She could have sworn the jar still tasted of blackberries.

"Hello, Bertie."

"Oh! Hello, Stella. I haven't seen you around for ages. How have you been keeping?"

Stella was once a large woman, but since she had contracted AIDS she had wasted away to a mere skeleton.

"I have good days and bad, but the nights are the hardest to get through," Stella replied.

"Have you been eating regular?" Bertie asked, concerned.

"When I can get out and about, I get a small bowl of soup. I can usually keep it down," Stella said.

"Have you had anything to eat today?" Bertie asked.

"No, not today. I've been panhandling all morning, trying to get enough money for bus fare. I promised Mom I'd visit her this week."

Bertie reached into her cup and pulled out a toonie and a loonie. She gently placed them in Stella's shaking hand. "Take this. It's enough for your fare."

"Thanks, Bertie," Stella said hoarsely.

Bertie sold four more pencils in less than half an hour. She counted her money, but she was still short one dollar. Another hour passed without any takers.

"Pencils for sale!" Bertie cried out, startling a man walking by. He reached into his pocket and pulled out two quarters. He threw them at Bertie's feet.

Bertie didn't even look down. "Pencils for sale!" she called.

"Well, aren't you even going to pick them up, old woman?" the man ridiculed.

Bertie turned slowly toward him and looked him straight in the face. "Sir! I sell pencils. I am not a beggar!" Bertie replied with dignity.

The man turned red in the face. "I'm sorry, I shouldn't have done that. I don't know what came over me. I've had a really bad day," he said.

"That's all right, everyone does. Lord knows I have. Here, have a free pencil," Bertie offered.

"Thanks. But I'd rather buy what you have left. How much are they?" he asked.

"It's by donation," replied Bertie.

The man gave her two toonies and took the remaining pencils.

"Have a good day, sir. And thanks." She had more than enough money for Anna's present and just enough time to get to the bookshop before it closed. Bertie took the money out of her cup and stuffed it in her pocket as she hurried down the street.

Anna would be so happy when she opened her gift, Bertie thought. Every time they had walked by the store, Anna had pressed her small face to the window to get a glimpse of the poetry book by Robert Louis Stevenson with colourful, pop-up pictures.

Anna had memorized two lines from one of the poems in the book. She knew if she repeated them often enough one day they would come true: "I have just to shut my eyes, to go sailing through the skies. To go sailing far away…."

Bertie realized she was walking too fast. Her breathing had become laboured and she felt quite dizzy. She rested her hand on the building next to her for support. A sharp pain ran up and down her left arm.

She lurched unsteadily toward a park bench and slumped down, exhausted. Her hands shook as she fumbled with the zipper of her knapsack, trying to get to her pills. The pain became more intense. Trying not to panic, she pressed down firmly and turned the lid. She put a pill under her tongue that burned as it dissolved, but the headache that always accompanied the pain grew even more severe.

Worried she wouldn't get to the store in this condition, she popped another pill under her tongue. She got up and took a few unsteady steps down the block. The store light was still on, but when she turned the doorknob it was locked. The sign in the window read: CLOSED. PLEASE CALL AGAIN. A tear slipped unchecked down her cheek.

"Bertie? Bertie, is that you?" asked Mr. Wilson. The bell over the doorway jingled merrily.

"Mr. Wilson? Thank goodness you're still here. I thought I had missed you."

"Now, it wouldn't be much of a birthday without a present, would it?" he laughed.

"No, indeed. Thank you for waiting," Bertie said.

Mr. Wilson took the wrapped package off the shelf and handed it to Bertie. She started counting out the money on the counter.

"No need for that, Bertie. I know you well enough to know it's all there. Are you feeling all right?"

"I had a bit of a spell a while ago, but I'm all right now," Bertie replied.

"Just wait until I get my coat and I'll drive you home."

"Why don't you join us? There will be plenty of cake for everyone. The more the merrier," said Bertie.

"Well, that sounds nice. Tell you what, we'll stop at a restaurant and I'll buy some Chinese food for the party."

"I can't say no to such a tempting offer. Could you get some of those little fortune cookies as well?"

◆

When Bertie and Mr. Wilson pulled up in front of the warehouse, Ben and Raven came running out.

"Bertie, are you all right? We were worried about you," Ben said anxiously.

"Just had a little spell, but I'm fine now. Did you get everything?" Bertie asked.

"Yes, everything is ready. I'll run over and get the kids and be back in five minutes. Raven, will you help Bertie finish the preparations?" he asked.

"Sure."

"Mr. Wilson has agreed to be our guest tonight," Bertie beamed.

After putting the final touches on the room Bertie, Raven and Mr. Wilson hid, wanting to surprise the children when they walked in.

"Happy birthday, Anna! Happy birthday, Robert!" they sang in chorus when the children entered a few minutes later.

To accommodate the festivities, two packing crates were joined end to end to form a longer table. Mr. Wilson had placed both large bags of Chinese food on the crates.

"Will you do the honours, Mr. Wilson?" Bertie asked.

"Why, I'd be delighted. Vegetable fried rice, mushroom egg foo young, sweet and spicy chicken, lettuce wrap, singapore chow mein, honey garlic pork and, last but not least, prawn crackers," he said as he pulled out container after container.

"Are there chopsticks?" Robert and Anna asked with excitement.

"Yes, and fortune cookies too," he answered.

The children had gone to a Chinese restaurant only once, on Bertie's birthday. The chopsticks had been the highlight of the evening.

"Don't forget the hats, Ben," Bertie reminded him.

He passed one to Mr. Wilson. He looked a little flustered, but was a good sport and put it on.

"Look, I can use chopsticks," Robert said excitedly. He picked up a piece of honey garlic pork. Almost instantly the chopsticks slipped sideways. The piece of pork flew in an arc only to land with a splash in Bertie's teacup.

"Oh my!" Bertie laughed. Raven giggled. Ben and the children laughed so hard tears streamed down their faces. Mr. Wilson grinned and winked at Bertie.

After everyone had had their fill Bertie announced, "It's time for cake."

"It's my turn to blow out the candles," Anna piped up.

"It is not! It's my turn. You did it last time," Robert whined.

"Now children. You can both blow them out at the same time," Bertie reminded them gently.

Anna gasped as the lone sparkler in the middle of the cake shot out a stream of white stars.

"All right. Now on the count of three you both blow out the candles. One, two, three," counted Ben.

Bertie cut a generous slice of cake for everyone. They ate with gusto. The children, for once, felt really full.

"Well, it must be time for the presents," Bertie announced.

"Presents! We're going to get presents too?" the children chimed.

Ben and Raven cleared the table.

"Can we keep up the bird and flower decorations forever and ever, Bertie?" the children begged.

Bertie nodded and placed a present in front of Anna and Ben did likewise for Robert.

Robert ripped his open and hooted with delight. "A harmonica! It's just what I wanted. Thank you."

"Aren't you going to open yours, Anna?" Bertie asked.

"I don't need a present, Bertie. You could have spent

the money on new shoes instead," she protested.

"Don't worry about that, sweetheart. I can put new cardboard in the soles when need be. Today is your special day, not mine. Now make my old heart happy and open the present," Bertie said kindly.

Anna undid the bow carefully; the bright red ribbon would be added to her special collection.

"The pop-up book. Oh thank you, Bertie! Thank you! Now, every night after supper, I can read it to you."

"I'll look forward to that. It's a good thing I taught you to read before my glasses broke."

"Can you play us a tune on your harmonica, Robert?" Raven asked.

"Sure. If Bertie will accompany me," he replied.

"I'm a bit winded. You go ahead," Bertie suggested.

After the festivities died down, Bertie asked Mr. Wilson for a private word. They talked secretly, deep in a serious conversation for almost half an hour. Finally, he put his coat and hat on, ready to leave.

"Goodnight, Bertie," he said as he tipped his hat to her. "Don't you worry none. They'll be fine. You have my word," promised Mr. Wilson.

Bertie retreated to a chair for a nap while Raven and Ben cleaned up. As they gathered up the dirty dishes and wrapping, they got to talking.

"Ben, how did you end up on the streets anyway?"

"I was born here."

"Born here?"

"Yeah. My grandma and grandpa had a big house near the corner of Georgia and Jackson. That was when

I was a baby. Grandpa worked at the railway yard."

"Why would anyone live in the downtown east side if they had a job?"

"In those days, it was a nice place to live. Everybody knew everybody else and there wasn't the crime there is now."

"So, what happened?"

"Grandpa was a switch man. One day when he was hurrying across the tracks in front of a train he lost his footing and tripped. He lost both legs in the accident and after that he went down hill. He died a few months later, only in his 50s. When my grandfather was alive, there was the odd wino or down-and-outer, but shortly after he died drug dealers started moving in and taking over the old neighbourhood. At least that's the way I remember it. The two events are forever connected in my mind."

"What about your grandma?"

"Once she was without her husband, she seemed to change for the worse. To top everything off, Mom…."

"Where *is* your mother?"

"She's in a home."

"What kind of home?"

"A home for the mentally ill. I go and visit her every now and then, but she doesn't know me. Her memory is ruined, from the cocaine. She'll be 36 on her next birthday."

"Will your mom ever get out of the hospital?"

"No. Her mind is destroyed. She can't look after herself," Ben explained.

"Was she always a drug addict?"

"No. I remember when I was about seven or eight she didn't drink *or* do drugs. But a year later everything changed. Her boyfriend at the time beat her up and I walked in on it one night. He grabbed her arm, spun her around and gave her a hard smack across the mouth. I saw red. I ran over and started pounding him with my fists and kicking him. He slapped me, then caught her by the hair and threw her down the stairs. He grabbed me by the arm and pushed both of us out the front door and slammed it shut behind us."

"Where did you go?"

"We didn't know where to go or what to do. We had been living in his house. It was the dead of winter and bitter cold. Mom hammered on the door begging for our coats. He flung open the door and threw them at us.

"I didn't know what I could say to comfort her. I wanted to say something, to protect her, but I was too young. She decided we should try her friend Cheryl, a cocktail waitress, who lived in a rundown tenement building. Mom slept on the couch and Cheryl made me a bed out of two old chairs. When I woke up, I wasn't sure where we were.

"When we went back to Mom's boyfriend's to get our clothes, we found them strewn on the front stairs and in the yard. A bottle of Mom's cheap perfume had broken. Our clothes, were doused in a sickeningly flowery smell. We wandered around, freeloading, and eventually she got a new boyfriend with a new habit and I was on my own. The rest is history.

"Anyway, enough of the sob story. I have to go over to Mrs. Larson's and help her get ready for bed. She can't manage by herself anymore. You wait here. I won't be long, then I'll walk you home. I'll get a Thermos of tea for Bertie while I'm over there."

Bertie, having heard her name, woke up out of the slumber she had retreated to after Mr. Wilson left.

"What's that? Did you call me, Ben?" Bertie asked.

"No, Bertie. I was just telling Raven I was going to get your Thermos filled."

"I could go for a spot of hot tea right now."

"See you in a few minutes," he shouted over his shoulder.

"Sorry I dozed off. What were you talking about?"

"I asked Ben about his mother."

"What did he tell you?"

"He told me about getting kicked out of her boyfriend's house, but it was a bit sketchy after that."

"He's been through a lot in his short life."

"How *did* she end up in a mental institution?"

"It's a tough story to tell. Darlene was little more than a kid herself. She found jobs, but couldn't seem to hold on to any. She had no training or skills."

"What happened?"

"Cheryl hooked up Darlene with a guy she knew. Darlene was innocent; she had been protected by her father while he was alive. The guy was only too happy to take Darlene on. He bought her new clothes, rented them a room and even gave her money for groceries. It was too good to be true. Everything seemed to be going well for a while. She made lots of money, though she wasn't allowed to keep much of it. She did manage to buy Ben a TV and stereo to keep him company while she was out. It bothered her that he was alone for so long while she was working," Bertie said.

"You mean he was left all alone in the apartment?"

"For hours at a time. To make matters worse, her drug habit escalated. Ben came home from school one day and discovered his TV was missing. Darlene had pawned it until 'her luck changed.' He never saw the TV again. A few weeks later, the stereo disappeared. He didn't even bother to ask where it went. By this time things were in a sorry state of affairs. Ben was reduced to trolling through the dumpsters to find food. That's why he has ordered Robert and Anna to stay out of trash bins.

"Darlene loved Ben, but she was at the mercy of the drugs. Everything was beyond her control, her son included. At first she'd come home every night. Then it got so bad she couldn't even remember where she lived from one day to the next. Ben started taking to the streets in search of her."

"Did he find her?"

"One night he found her facedown on the street, passed out cold. Ben put his tiny arm around her and laid down beside her. In the morning the police found them there, sound asleep. The police arrested her and welfare took Ben away," Bertie sighed.

"Did she ever get Ben back?" Raven asked.

"It took quite a while. She went cold turkey, but they wouldn't let her have him unless she could prove she was a fit parent. She held down a job for a while and regained custody, but it didn't last. No matter how hard she tried to quit the drugs, she couldn't stop. It didn't take long for her to hit the streets again. She started locking him in the room at night so he wouldn't wander the streets looking for her."

"But what if there was a fire? What if he was sick?" Raven asked.

"She wasn't thinking rationally. She couldn't imagine anything beyond the next fix. By then, she was pretty much a 24-7 girl."

"What do you mean '24-7 girl'?"

"It's a term for the girls who work 24 hours a day, seven days a week. They've got the habit so bad they seldom sleep. Some can go for as long as four days before they literally collapse. Their life, if you can call it that, is one miserable cycle. They think of nothing more than scoring and fixing. Their bosses wouldn't want it any other way."

"What happened to Ben?"

"The neighbours got suspicious and called the police. The cops found the room locked and broke in. There was nothing in the room except a dirty old mattress and a threadbare blanket, a rotten plate of food, a half-empty water bottle and a chamber pot that was overflowing. The stench was so offensive it made one of the officers gag. It was enough to convince the social workers to take Ben away permanently.

"At first they couldn't find Darlene to notify her. But they soon discovered that she had been admitted to the hospital for an overdose. She's been in a mental institution ever since."

"How did Ben come to live with you?" Raven inquired.

"Well, he wouldn't stay at any foster home. He kept running away. I met him on the streets and we became friends. When he ran away, he came here, to visit me. I was scared that one day he would run away for good and that would be the end of it, so I invited him to live with me. When you're born on the skids, I guess it feels like home," Bertie offered.

"You've been looking after him ever since?"

"I guess you could say that. But it's mutual. It was the same with Robert and Anna. I look after them, they looks after me. We're a family."

SEVEN

Neon light flooded the water-soaked streets slick with the hypnotic swish of cars plowing through puddles.

"Is something wrong, Ben?" Raven asked while they were walking back to her room.

"Huh? No, I was just thinking about Bertie. She had another spell tonight and tried to cover it up," Ben answered.

"Maybe you can convince her to go to the clinic tomorrow," Raven suggested.

"I'll have to. She can't go on like this."

They stopped in front of her building. " Well, here we are. Goodnight."

"Goodnight, Ben. I really enjoyed myself tonight. Thanks." She walked up the steps and checked for a message on the bulletin board by the telephone:

nothing. Raven was careful not to alert her lecherous neighbour. He was bound to harass her if he heard her in the hall.

She sat on the edge of the bed, rereading the diary entries and trying to make a list of clues, other places to look. When she turned to the back of the diary, she realized there were a number of undated entries she'd missed; the pages had been stuck together. She pored over them desperately now.

Dear Diary

I'm still having trouble sleeping and one minute I'm happy, the next I'm depressed. I can't seem to concentrate. I have to quit the coke. I have to be stronger. I have to be…anything but this.

Dear Diary

Lonnie has started packing a gun. When I asked him why he needed one, he said a gang of Honduran drug dealers were selling rock cocaine in his territory. They were also trying to move in on his girls. He said their girls pipeline the drugs across the border; they work a circuit between Portland, Vegas and Dallas. But Lonnie could use the gun on one of us just as easily….

Dear Diary

Lonnie and I went for a long walk by ourselves. He told me how much he needed me and said that tomorrow we'd take two vans out to

Coquitlam and Port Moody to recruit. He told me I'd be a big help to him if I told the kids how exciting life was on the streets. He wanted me to make sure I mentioned that down here there were no rules, just plenty of fun.

Dear Diary

Lonnie and I cruised by some schoolgrounds and then he dropped me off and told me to get to know the kids. I chatted with them for a while and invited them to the arcade after school. I said they could play all the games they wanted, free, just like Lonnie told me to. Before school got out, we cruised by again. Three girls and one boy came over and Lonnie offered them cigarettes laced with heroin. He told them about the huge arcades in Vancouver. He got them totally pumped, so they came along. On the way back to the city, I found out the boy was an athlete and one of the girls was an A-student, but they were bored and kept saying they had nothing to lose. They were tired of being "good kids" and said they wanted to live a little, to show their parents they could do what they wanted.

Dear Diary

The next morning, the kids were gone. Lonnie said they were homesick, so Jake took them back in the middle of the night. They were too young anyway.

Dear Diary

There's a big party tonight. Lonnie hasn't been around for a couple of days. Every morning I resolve to go home, but by evening I've changed my mind. I need help. Even if I do break free, will Lonnie…?

Dear Diary

I want to go home, but how will I tell Mom and Dad I've failed? I left for the city with such grand plans, but I haven't accomplished anything. Doing drugs is not an accomplishment. I don't think I can face them. They would take one look at me and know what I've become. My "friends" are rough and Dora scares me. She doesn't like me, but as long as Lonnie does, I'm safe. Dora beat up another girl, broke her arm to show her who was boss. I don't want to hang around with them anymore, but I'm afraid to say so. Why did I ever get involved with them?

If Raven didn't hear from her father or find Marcie by tomorrow morning, she didn't know what she would do. She felt so helpless; she could hardly wait until daylight to start searching again.

Just as Raven was dropping off to sleep, sometime around midnight, a gunshot tore through the silence, followed in rapid succession by two more. They sounded like they came from somewhere behind her building. A few minutes later shrill sirens pierced the night air, increased in volume, then stopped abruptly. Somebody nearby must have called 9-1-1. Out the window, Raven could see the police and paramedics standing beside the body of a young man lying prone on the street. Tendrils of blood trickled down his shirtfront. A small bag lay beside him.

Raven could hear the paramedics talking as they examined the body and prepared to transport the man to the hospital. Meanwhile, the police searched for i.d. but found none. They said the only clue to the man's identity was the initials on his belt buckle: J.L.

The victim whispered something feebly.

"Listen, he's trying to say something," the police officer said. He leaned closer, straining to hear. "Sounds like he's calling for mercy."

"We'd better move him or he'll be DOA." The paramedic transferred him to a stretcher and loaded him into the ambulance. It speed off with the lights flashing and the siren blaring.

A few moments later the downstairs door burst open with a bang and footsteps bounded up the stair-well. Raven heard pounding on the neighbour's door and then, "Open up! It's the police!"

"What do you want?" the neighbour sneered.

"We're looking for a gunman. A man was shot out back. Is anyone else in the room with you?" the police-man inquired.

"No, just me," he declared defensively.

"Have you been out tonight?"

"No. I was here all night. Hey, man, don't look at me. You've got the wrong guy."

"We'll be back for further questioning. Don't go anywhere and be prepared to offer an alibi. We'll need to know everything you can tell us. If you see or hear anything, call us immediately," the officer said. The police asked other tenants in the building the same questions, going door to door.

When they came to her door, Raven answered all the questions and then thought to inquire about her sister. Could the shooting be related? The officer had no information to connect Marcie's disappearance with the gunshots, but he promised someone would keep her posted. He took down a description, looked at the picture and scribbled all the details in his notepad. His words were small consolation and she spent the rest of the night tossing and turning, imagining the worst.

◆

Marcie grew tired of waiting for J.L. to return to his apartment. She'd been expecting him since midnight. She decided to go back to her old address, to get the black book herself and see if J.L. had left her a note.

But she didn't get any farther than the yellow police tape that cordoned off a section of asphalt behind the building. It was speckled with dried blood. A crowd of bikers stood smoking and talking behind the American Hotel. She heard them say something about, "some guy buying it earlier." He was alive, but barely, they said. She had to phone the hospitals; it might be J.L.!

If she made an anonymous call it might reveal the victim's name and status.

She sifted through her pockets searching for a quarter and then looked for a phone that hadn't been vandalized. Once in a booth, her fingers shaking as she inserted the quarter in the slot, she dialled the number for Vancouver Gerneral.

"Did a J.L. come in this morning?" Marcie asked.

"You will have to give me a name. I'm afraid people aren't registered under their initials," the receptionist replied sarcastically in a nasal voice.

"His first name is Johnny."

"I must have a surname. There are a number of patients with that first name."

"He was brought in with a gunshot wound," Marcie stammered.

"You must be talking about Johnny Latimer. Does he have blond hair?" the receptionist asked.

"Yes, that's him. Is he all right?"

"Are you related?"

"No, I'm his girlfriend."

"I'm afraid I can't release that information."

She would try again in an hour, hope for another nurse, maybe pretend she was family. She would have to go in person if she didn't get anywhere. In the meantime she could at least carry on with their plan: she would go to Lonnie's warehouse on the pier and confront him about J.L.'s sister. She'd been there before with Lonnie and had waited in the car while he'd made his business deals. It would be dangerous, given Lonnie's mood the last time she saw him, but she owed J.L., especially now. He must have found the book; that was probably why he had been shot in the first place — possession of Lonnie's property. Lonnie must have suspected Jilly of jacking the books and come back to scour the apartment when he ran into J.L. She would have to risk confronting him — lives might depend on it.

◆

Within half an hour Marcie was hunched behind crates on the dock. The warehouse was on a pier facing a large ship moored in the dockyards. Some of the ship's crew walked past. One muttered something about the kids on board making good fish bait. He said he was glad they would be pushing off that night.

So it was true! And Melissa might be among them! Marcie would have to go aboard. She would have a better chance of sneaking on if the ship wasn't so heavily guarded. She spotted one sentry walking along the deck, a second sentry on the bow.

"Hey, Manny. I don't feel too good. Is it OK if I go get some shut eye?" shouted the second sentry.

"Yeah, sure. Go ahead. Why'd we get stuck with this shift anyway?" the other sentry complained.

"Give me a shout in a couple of hours, will you?"

The second sentry finished his cigarette, flicked the butt over the railing, stretched and slowly walked toward the stern. Marcie sprinted toward the gangplank and tripped over a raised metal lip between the gangplank and the gangway. She grabbed the railing, barely managing to keep herself from falling, and tiptoed across to the starboard side of the ship to hide beside the smokestack. There was a wooden door a few steps away from where she was huddled. She had to get in there.

She turned the doorknob gently — unlocked. As the door closed silently behind her she descended a steep set of steps that opened onto a long hallway. At the end of the hall was a large metal door with a glass window at eye level. Hesitantly, she peered inside. Her eyes widened in alarm. Inside the room about 20 teenagers were handcuffed to their cots. Marcie jumped back from the window and flattened herself against the wall. She didn't want them to spot her. They might cry out either in alarm or for help.

"Hey, you. What are you doing there?" growled an angry voice. A huge silhouette loomed menacingly at the far end of the hallway.

Marcie's eyes widened in fear.

"Stop or I'll shoot!" he bellowed.

◆

It was mid-morning when Raven walked down the hall to the bathroom, turned on the light and began to take clean clothes out of her bag. As she bathed she listened to morning noises signalling a new day … alarm clocks ringing, doors opening and closing, radio static and the 10 a.m. news. The smell of freshly brewed coffee drifted down the hallway. Raven was tired and hungry. She dressed, packed her small knapsack and trudged down the stairs.

On the last step she tripped on a tiny book. She flipped through it briefly; it was some sort of address book containing numbers and names. There was no lost and found in the building so she decided she'd look through it for the owner's name and then try to call later to let the owner know she had found it.

She went back to the restaurant at the bus depot, because the food was cheap, and ordered an egg sandwich and hot chocolate. As she ate, she flipped through the newly found book. On its pages were columns with times, dates and names; beside the names were prices.

Just before Raven left the bus depot, she placed a call to Frank's store, but no one answered. She decided to stop off at the free clinic and see if Ben was there yet. He had said he was going to take Bertie today. She prayed he had a new lead.

"Hi, Ben," she said when she spotted him.

"Hi, Raven. Any news? Did you reach your folks this morning?"

"No, there was no answer. I guess all I can do is check out the strip again and take my chances."

"I'd go with you, but I have to wait for Bertie."

"How is she?"

"I'm really worried. It's not like her to volunteer to come to the clinic. Usually, I have to hound her for days before she'll give in."

"I'm sure she'll be fine. I better get going. Give Bertie my love and we'll hook up at your place later."

Raven walked toward the strip. She was halfway down the block when a woman striding toward her with long black hair and a black leather jacket reached into her pocket for a syringe. She ripped the plastic packet open with her teeth and had the needle out in three strides.

Another woman, at the far end of the block, carried a heavy cardboard box, put it on the sidewalk, stood up and positioned her arms as if to waltz. Raven dubbed her Waltzing Mathilda. Suddenly, the woman bent in two, grasping her stomach. Her head slowly raised as her mouth opened wide in a silent scream. Raven overheard a guy nearby say, "She's hurting, hurting real bad for a fix."

"Hey, Miss Priss. What you snooping around for?"

"Par...pardon? Are you talking to me?" Raven replied, turning around quickly to face her accuser.

"Of course I'm talking to you. Who else? Or are you too good to talk to someone in a wheelchair? Why are you down here anyway? You don't belong on these streets," he snapped.

"I'm looking for my sister."

"Most of the kids that come snooping around down here are just out for a few laughs, so if you're legit, let's see a picture."

Raven held out the photograph of Marcie.

"No, I haven't seen her. She working the strip?"

"Working the strip? What do you mean?" Raven gulped.

"Good grief, girl, you're about as green as..." he

began. "What will you give me if I help you find her?" he said slyly.

"Give you? Like a reward or something?"

"Money. You know about money, don't you?"

"I guess I could give you $10," Raven offered.

"Ten dollars! Ten stinking dollars! Don't do me any favours. How much is your sister worth anyway? Doesn't sound like you want to find her that badly," he barked.

"I do. I just have to be very careful with my money. I'm saving to go to university," Raven said plaintively.

"An egghead as well. Yeah, well I'm waiting to go to university myself. Just waiting for my scholarship to come through," he guffawed. "How much money do you have?" he asked gruffly.

"I have about $150 left," Raven said honestly.

He thumped both fists on the arms of his wheel-chair. "Are you nuts? You don't tell someone how much money you've got. Not ever."

"But, but you asked me," Raven said tearfully.

"That doesn't mean you have to tell me," he snarled.

Raven began to sob — what did he want from her?

"What the hell are you snivelling about?" he demanded.

"I'm not used to people talking to me like this," she gulped.

"You think *I'm* nasty? I'm *living* it, day after stinking day. I've been stabbed, robbed and beaten. They left me for dead. I lost the use of both legs. Don't tell *me* what nasty is, kid."

"I'm sorry."

"Ah, what are *you* sorry for? You didn't do anything. Tell you what, if it'll shut you up, I'll take you over to Toots' place."

"Who's Toots?"

"She runs the Green Room."

"What's that?"

"Uh…uh, sort of a massage parlour, you know, a pad."

"Do you think she might have seen my sister?"

"Well, if anyone has, Toots has. She gets around."

"OK. Let's go."

"You can give me the $10 now."

"But you haven't helped me find her yet."

"Well, you can look at it as a kind of down payment. Besides, I can get 10 glasses of draft with that at the pub. Come on. You might as well push me; it will be faster."

"How far is this Green Room?"

"Just down Hastings. And another thing, you can call me Norm. What's yours?"

"Raven. What's the matter with that man across the street? He's shaking all over. Is he having a convulsion or something?"

"He's doing what's called 'the chicken.' Whatever you do, don't stare. Keep on going," Norm warned. The man's girlfriend, standing beside him, threw a beer bottle at them. Luckily, her aim was off and it fell far short of its mark.

"What thet hell are you staring at? You've never seen anybody throw a fit before? I'll fix you good!" she screamed.

"Get us out of here quick," Norm barked.

Raven didn't need to be prodded. She pushed the wheelchair along at record speed and didn't look back.

"Come back here. I'll give you both a beating you won't forget!" she screamed.

"Is she chasing us?" Norm said nervously.

Raven glanced over her shoulder to double-check. "No. It's OK"

"Well, I guess you learned your lesson: don't stare, or point, at anyone. Many of these guys used to be in mental institution. A few years ago, the government closed it down and most of the 4,000 patients had nowhere to go but the streets. Now a lot of them call the skids home. They survive from one day to the next the best they can."

In the next block they came to a vacant lot cordoned off with razor wire and mesh fencing. A tiny woman stood in front of the fence dressed only in shorts and a thin cotton T-shirt. She picked at her scalp with torn fingernails and had a wound on her leg, a knife or razor cut with its stitches pulled loose. Norm spotted her before Raven did.

"For god's sake, look the other way. It's Tiny Tina. Just pretend you don't see her," Norm instructed.

"What's the matter with her? Why is she tearing at her scalp like that?"

"She's got what the doctors call 'cocaine psychosis'."

"What's that?"

"She imagines there are bugs crawling under her skin. She scratches to try to dig them out."

"Can't somebody help her?"

"I guess you have to want help before you can get it. The pull of the drugs is much stronger than the will to survive. There's not much anyone can do for her. Anyway, Toots' place is just up ahead."

They stopped at the next big building and Raven looked up a long flight of stairs. "How are you going to get up there?"

"I don't need to go up. Pass me my cane." He banged the cane sharply on the stairwell wall. The door at the top swung open and the Green Room's bouncer filled the doorframe.

"What you want?" he growled.

Raven's eyes widened in shock; he was huge.

"Toots. She here?"

"Yeah."

"Well, this kid needs to talk to her."

Raven wasn't so sure she wanted to, now that she knew who she'd be dealing with.

"Yeah. Send her up."

"Go on. Just tell her you're a friend of mine," Norm prodded.

Raven swallowed hard and climbed the stairs to the landing.

"Wait here," the bouncer commanded. He left the door slightly ajar. Raven spotted a number of cubicles inside, cordoned off by shiny brass rods suspended from the ceiling. Plush green velvet drapes hung from each rod. A short, stocky woman came to the door. Raven had never seen anyone wear so much makeup.

"What do you want, girlie? You looking for work?"

"No, ma'am. I'm looking for my sister, Marcie. Norm thought you might help me."

"You with Norm? Why didn't you say so?" Norm waved at Toots, who waddled down the stairs. "Norm. I haven't seen you in weeks. You want somebody to carry you upstairs?"

"No, not today. I'm helping this kid look for her sister. Raven, show Toots the picture."

"I've seen her around, but not lately. She hangs out with a bad crowd, that one."

"Do you know anyone who might know where she is?"

"No, afraid not. I better get back to work. Good to see you, Norm." Toots waddled back up the stairs and disappeared behind the curtains while Norm spun around in his chair and tried to think of plan B.

"I know a guy named Pierre who makes it his business to know what's going on. If you want to buy or sell something, he'll put you in touch with the right people. You know what I mean?" he said guardedly.

Raven nodded while she pushed Norm along the sidewalk. She stopped at the curb, waiting for the light to change. A long white limousine raced through both the red light and the crosswalk and almost hit them. Norm cursed wild drivers under his breath. Raven crossed cautiously, visibly shaken.

"Turn left here. It's the third house on the right side of the street."

A few minutes later, Raven stopped in front of a

trim house unlike the others on the block.

"Go up the stairs and knock," Norm instructed.

Raven knocked on the door, but there was no answer. A note read: BACK TOMORROW.

A man vaulted up the steps of the house next door, counted out some bills, folded the bills in half, then stuffed them through the mail slot. He stood waiting. Seconds later a small hand passed a packet through the same mail slot. The man grabbed it and scurried away.

"What was that? What was he doing?"

"He was making a buy. An old woman lives in that house. Her daughter ran off a couple of years back and left a boy for her to raise. She's blind and crippled from a run-in with her last supplier. The little guy is her legs; he does the deals through the mail slot."

"Why don't the authorities do something?"

"They will, if they catch them. The police are busy night and day with bigger crimes and so far they've avoided being caught."

"How old is he?"

"I reckon about six or seven years old," Norm replied. "Listen kid, do you know anyone your sister hung out with?"

"Marcie hung out around the Balmoral Hotel with a guy named Lonnie," Raven said, exasperated.

"Lonnie?" Norm asked, recognition flashing across his craggy features.

"Yes. Do you know him?"

"I know *of* him. I don't know him personally. He's as sly as a fox, that one. He gets everybody to do his dirty work so that if they get caught he just waltzes away free as a bird. If anybody crosses him they won't live to do it again, that's for sure. I do know he has a warehouse down on the docks."

"Do you know where, exactly?"

"Somewhere around Campbell Avenue."

"Well, that's something. I think I'll just take a look down there and keep my eyes and ears open. It's my only lead at the moment."

"I'll be seeing you, then. I've got drinking plans this afternoon provided I make a bit of cash," he said hopefully.

Raven said goodbye and handed him $10. Norm waved as he watched her walk north toward the water.

EIGHT

Raven glanced at the graffiti-covered wall beside her. Her eyes were riveted to the bottom left-hand corner: a bear paw print. It had to be some sort of sign or talisman to guide her to her sister. She turned the corner, heading east toward the grain silos on the waterfront and crossed the concrete bridge toward the pier. The street abruptly stopped at Campbell Avenue, where dozens of railway tracks, mud oozing from the base of the ties, veered left and right. Five Chinese men walked toward her carrying on their backs heavy baskets filled with fish.

A number of abandoned aluminum buildings stood on the far side of the tracks, coated in dirt. Seagulls roosted on their window ledges. Inside the first building, people wearing white aprons and black gum-boots filleted fish. They iced the fillets, then put them in boxes stacked for delivery. The floor was glossy with silvery fish scales and running water. Raven continued down the dock, listening to the seagulls fighting over fish guts. The other warehouses had heavy padlocks on the doors, but the last warehouse door she came to was slightly ajar.

A raspy voice from inside barked out orders, "Vern, get to work. This shipment has to be ready to sail tonight. We're getting a good price for the bear gall bladders, hides and paws."

"How much, Stan?" another man she couldn't see, but supposed was Vern, asked.

"For this load, I'd say around a quarter of a million dollars," Stan ventured.

Vern let out a long whistle, but stopped abruptly when he heard a noise outside. He didn't want anyone sniffing around, so he went to investigate.

Raven was so intent on spying on them she didn't see a man sneak up behind her. A huge hand grabbed her arm, roughly twisting it behind her back.

"What you doing here?" Vern snarled.

She recognized him! He was one of the poachers she had seen in the campground near home the day before she left for the city!

◆

Marcie's small body lay crumpled on the cold tile wheelhouse floor. The gash on her head throbbed and the pain intensified as she struggled to get up. She felt a hand on her shoulder and turned her head to face a slight, pale, blonde girl about her own age.

"Are you all right?" the girl asked.

"Who are you?" Marcie blurted. "Where are we? Why are we here? Did they capture you too?"

"I live on the ship. I help the cook with the meals. Why are *you* here?"

"My name is Marcie. I was looking for my friend's sister when they caught me and tossed me in here."

"What's your friend's name?" the girl hedged.

"J.L."

"J.L.! You know J.L.? He's my brother! I'm Melissa!"

"Thank goodness, I found you. How long have you been here? Did they hurt you? What happened?" Marcie blurted, both relieved and terrified.

"It's a long story. A few months ago some men came by my school driving expensive cars, flashing money around, dressed to the nines. They said they were from Vancouver and looking for a good time. It was a change from the local scene and besides they invited us to parties and paid for everything. After a few nights of the good life, they said they wanted to hire us to work in the city — told us we could make a killing. They said we'd soon have enough money to buy anything we wanted.

"Most of us were bored and hadn't found summer jobs and were fighting with our parents. School was almost out and we would have been looking for work in the next few weeks anyway. We packed our bags and after a final blast in town we piled into two cars and headed for Vancouver. We figured we'd call our parents once we had an address and had started work.

When we got to Hope, two vans transporting kids from towns in the Interior joined us.

"In Vancouver they separated us by age. The younger children were ordered to walk the "Kiddie Stroll" at Franklin and Victoria and then they sent the older group to a big apartment downtown. They held a party that night, but spiked the drinks so that we were unconscious while they transported us to the locked rooms aboard this ship. They could have done anything; we were defenceless.

"I remember waking up on the ship, shackled to a bed in a locked cell. I was terrified. There was no telling where we would end up or what they would do to us. Eventually, we learned that some would be weeded out to go to a training camp in Alberta and then they'd be rerouted through Vancouver. The group I was with was going to be sent to some port in Asia via Seattle and Hawaii. When the ship docked in Asia, the others were sold at a private auction. I was sick, so they couldn't sell me. The cook said he could use a hand in the kitchen, so I was spared. He nursed me back to health and I've been working on the boat ever since. They keep me under constant supervision. They don't want a snitch who could try to make a break for it."

"When is this load set to sail?" Marcie asked.

"The ship sails tonight. Where is J.L.? Why isn't he here? Is he OK?" Melissa said, worried.

"J.L. was shot. I think he's going to pull through, but I don't know for sure."

"It's my fault, isn't it? He came to the city to look

for me. I could be responsible for my brother's death. If J.L. died, I wouldn't be able to live with myself. I couldn't face my family," Melissa sobbed.

"He won't die, but if he did, it would be even more important that you go home. Would you let your brother's sacrifice be in vain? He would want you to be safe," Marcie said firmly.

"I know you're right. Why did I ever run away in the first place?"

Marcie put her arms around Melissa as they sat huddled on the floor, each of them wishing she was at the hospital with J.L. and that all of this was just a bad dream.

◆

Vern had Raven by the arm, but not for long. She kicked him as hard as she could and took off running.

"Stop!" he yelled after her.

Stan came running out of the warehouse. "What's going on?" he demanded.

"It's that brat, the salal picker we ran into in Egmont. She was spying on us. I didn't think you'd want any witnesses," Vern said, rubbing his sore leg.

"Forget her, there's no time. We need to get the cash from Lonnie. Let's load before there's more trouble," Stan ordered.

Vern hobbled back inside the warehouse. They quickly packed the contraband, loaded the boxes onto a dolly and wheeled it to the truck parked out back. Vern hoisted the boxes onto the truck and jumped in.

Raven realized Stan had said "Lonnie" — it had to be the same guy from Marcie's journal! Maybe they would lead her to her sister. Raven watched from her vantage point behind some nearby crates as they drove to a pier a short distance away, parked on the dock beside a ship and walked up the gangplank.

Raven followed on foot and crouched near their truck. A few minutes later they walked off the ship with a deckhand, involved in a heated discussion.

"Why can't you give us our money?" Stan demanded.

"I told you, the captain has the money and I'm not supposed to leave my post," the deckhand said.

"Well, I want it and fast," Stan yelled.

"I'll take you to him," the deckhand snapped.

Raven saw a cell phone on the seat of Stan's truck only a few feet away. She reached in the window, grabbed it and dialled 9-1-1.

"State what your emergency is, your location and your name," the operator said.

"I've uncovered a smuggling ring operating at the Vancouver dockyards. I am at the first pier east of Campbell Avenue. My name is Raven. Please send the police immediately."

"We'll send someone right away. Do not attempt to deal with the situation yourself," the operator said, but Raven had already hung up and was halfway up the gangplank before the operator finished talking.

She searched the ship from one end to the other, careful to avoid the crew. She walked stealthily from door to door, jiggling the locked handles in the hope that one would be open. She cupped her hands around her eyes to peer into dark windows. At the wheelhouse window she jumped back in fright; her sister's face was looking back at her! They both started whispering through the thick glass at once. Marcie strained to say, "Raven, is that you? What are you doing here?"

"Thank goodness I've found you! What a relief! How do I get you out of there?"

Melissa's face appeared at the window as well. "There's a spare key on a nail beside the stove in the galley. The same key will open the room directly below us where the other kids are being held. Do you know where the galley is?" Melissa asked.

"Yes. I passed it a few minutes ago. I'll be right back," Raven promised.

She ran into the galley, grabbed the key and raced toward Marcie's room. She vaulted up the steps of the wheelhouse, unlocked the door and threw her arms around her sister.

"Raven, is it really you? How did you find us?" Marcie asked, relieved but incredulous.

"I've been staying in your room. I read your diary and you wrote something about a dream and a pier and someone named Lonnie. It was a long shot, but I was desperate. On the way, I met a guy named Norm who knew Lonnie had a warehouse down here. I overheard some poachers talk about doing business with the same guy, so I followed them onto the boat. I called the police before I boarded, but Lonnie or the crew might discover us before the reinforcements arrive. You two get off the ship so you can tell the police where we are if we're not off ourselves by then," Raven said.

"But we can't leave you and the others. Only the sentries have keys for their handcuffs and it could be dangerous…" Melissa protested.

"Listen, there's no time to argue. Go!" Raven ordered. Marcie and Melissa hurried down the gangplank and hid behind crates on the pier, awaiting the sirens and patrol cars.

Raven raced back downstairs to the crew's quarters. She entered and tiptoed over to a sleeping sentry. His keys were fastened to his belt loop. She unclipped the key ring without waking him and raced to the room where the hostages were being held, praying one of the keys would be the right one to set them free.

"I'm here to help you escape. Don't ask questions, just pass this key around to unlock the handcuffs and be ready to run," Raven ordered when she burst through the door.

"How do we know we can trust you?" one boy asked. Another 20 faces looked to her for proof. They were regular kids, like those she went to school with, despite their disheveld appearance and tired, strung-out expressions.

"It doesn't really matter if you can trust me or not. I don't see how you could be in any more trouble than you're in now, do you?" Raven pointed out.

◆

Marcie and Melissa peered cautiously over the top of the crates. Five men were walking up the pier toward the ship.

Marcie recognized Lonnie's tall frame, but didn't know the other four men. When she looked up at the ship, she saw Raven in plain view, the hostages walking noiselessly in single file behind her. They were sitting ducks!

At that moment, four patrol cars rounded the corner and screeched to a stop at the pier. Lonnie and the others reached for their guns. An officer jumped out, pointed his gun and yelled, "Hold your fire. Put your weapons on the ground and lie facedown!"

All five men fell to the ground and were soon swarmed by officers and placed in handcuffs. The police loaded them into the cruisers and read them their rights. Meanwhile, the port authorities seized the ship, including the captain and crew, and ushered the teenagers to safety. They would have to call their parents and give their testimonies at the station.

The officer who had investigated J.L.'s shooting the night before took their testimonies and remembered Raven. After taking down the details of Melissa's and Marcie's stories, he passed on the news that J.L. was out of danger and recovering. Both Melissa and Marcie planned to visit him as soon as they finished the paperwork at the station. As long as Lonnie, his brother and their goons were put behind bars, the girls would finally be safe.

◆

Later that afternoon, Melissa phoned home, but the phone just rang and rang. She thought this was odd; they were rarely out in the evening.

"I should phone home too," Marcie said to Raven.

"The store won't be open until tomorrow morning," Raven said.

"Right, I forgot about that. Let's take a bus to the hospital, then. I hope they'll let us see J.L."

"It's after visiting hours," Melissa objected.

"Well, maybe we can bend the rules. If we're lucky someone will look the other way and let us visit for a few minutes," Marcie replied.

During the ride to the hospital, Melissa and Marcie fell silent, both thinking about J.L. and how much he meant to each of them. He just had to pull through.

"We're here," Raven said as she got off at the Cambie Street stop. They went west on 10th Street until they got to the main doors. The trio walked quietly toward the receptionist's desk.

"Could you please tell me which room Johnny Latimer is in?" Melissa said.

"It's after visiting hours," the receptionist said. "Have you come from out of town?"

"Yes," Melissa said, recalling her ordeal and her hometown in the Okanagan.

"Well, I guess you can see him for just a minute. He's in intensive care. Go down the hall to the end and turn left. And remember, just two minutes," she said kindly.

Marcie and Melissa walked down the darkened hall uncertainly. They found the room and inched the door open. He lay so still, hooked up to oxygen and IV. Next to the bed, a woman stirred in a chair, her face partly covered by a blanket.

"Can I help you? What do you want?" a muffled voice asked groggily, her head still turned away from them.

"Mom, is that you?" Melissa cried in astonishment.

"Melissa! Oh god, I thought you were dead!" her mother said, both relieved and shocked.

Melissa raced over to her mother and threw her arms around her. "Oh Mom, I'm sorry…so sorry. Can you ever forgive me?"

"You're back now, sweetheart. That's all that really matters. I'm so relieved. I must call your father right away. You know, we never stopped praying J.L. would be able to find you," she said as she stroked Melissa's hair.

"Mel…Melissa," groaned J.L.

"I'm here, Johnny. I'm all right. Marcie is here too," Melissa said softly, introducing Raven and Marcie to her mother.

"I think we should go out in the hall and talk. Johnny needs his sleep," Mrs. Latimer suggested.

As soon as she closed the door, Melissa confronted her mother with a barrage of questions. "How is he, Mom? What's the matter with him? When did you get here? What do the doctors say? Can we stay with him even though it's after visiting hours?"

"Hold on. One question at a time. The specialist said J.L. is going to live, but the bullet hit his spine. The doctor doesn't know yet if the paralysis is temporary or if he'll ever recover. The next few days will be crucial. Even if he does get back the use of his legs, he's looking at months of therapy."

"This is all my fault. If he hadn't come searching for me, he never would have been shot," Melissa wailed.

"Listen Melissa, he needs you to be strong. He needs all of us to help him through this ordeal. The important thing is you're both OK," Marcie said calmly.

Marcie and Raven left Melissa and Mrs. Latimer to catch up on the months they'd been apart and the day's dramatic events. After exchanging their home addresses and phone numbers so that they could keep in touch, Marcie asked for a few minutes alone with J.L. She held his hand tenderly, then kissed him good-bye before slipping silently out the door.

NINE

The next day, Raven looked on as the last wires on the totem pole were cut. It was a hot, sunny day and the park was crowded with street people who had come to attend the memorial ceremony.

"We're here today to dedicate this totem to those who have died on the downtown lower east side streets. You are invited to take some flowers out of the bucket here and lay them at the foot of the pole. You are also welcome to say a few words on behalf of those you have lost," said an official speaking through a red-and-white bullhorn.

Men, women and children who lived on the street filed forward to speak into the bullhorn. They remembered wives, mothers, sisters, brothers and friends who had overdosed, been murdered, fallen ill to AIDS, disease or hypothermia or disappeared without a trace. In most cases, those who had died were the survivor's only family. Many of those dead were women, women who had been killed on the job by the men they worked for or for unpaid drug debts. Bodies the police recovered on the streets that couldn't be identified were often buried in unmarked graves.

A man at the head of the line stepped forward, his hands trembling visibly as he reached for the flower bucket. "I'd like to…" he choked, then stopped to clear his throat. "I'd like to remember my dear wife, Rosa, and her sister. They got into some bad stuff last winter, drugs that were too pure. They overdosed on the spot. They were good women who never hurt anybody. All of you, everyone who knew them, can testify to that." He stood to one side with his head bowed.

A young woman began, "I'd like to say a few words about my twin sister, Dee. She was murdered a couple of months ago. She was only 26, full of fun and my closest friend. There are over 20 women missing in the downtown east side, yet no one is doing anything about it. Why don't the police — why doesn't the law — protect *us*? Don't we have rights the same as everybody else? My sister was strangled like a rag doll — no one knows how long her body lay in a dumpster before somebody found her…" she sobbed.

Raven was finding it difficult to swallow and she struggled to keep from crying. She saw Anna and Robert come forward, but Ben and Bertie were nowhere in sight. Raven hadn't had a chance to talk to them since reuniting with Marcie.

Anna held her brother's small hand while she picked up two bunches of flowers, passing one bouquet to Robert and gripping the other as if for strength.

"My brother and I want to say a few words about Bertie. Bertie was like a mother to us. Our whole family died in a fire a couple of years ago. Bertie found us wandering the streets and took us in. She did the best she could for us, kept us fed and warm and showered us with love. She died late last night. Her huge heart just up and gave out," Anna whispered.

Robert placed his flowers at the base of the pole and wiped away a tear with his fist. "I love you more than chocolate, Bertie," he cried out.

His sister hugged him tightly against her.

Tears streamed down Raven's face. What would happen to the children now? What would they do without Bertie? At that moment she spotted Ben striding across the park. He knelt down in front of the children, gathering both of them in his arms.

"Raven, hurry up or we'll miss the bus," Marcie yelled from across the street.

Raven couldn't leave without hugging Ben and the kids and telling them how much their help meant to her, how badly she felt about Bertie.

She gave Ben her address in Egmont and promised that they would see each other again and write in the meantime. Her heart gave a lurch as she looked back and met Ben's eyes. Raven knew how relieved she was to leave the shadow of the downtown east side, but would Ben be so lucky?

◆

Raven stood in line at the depot to buy two tickets for home. Marcie stood beside her leaning on her suitcase, shakily.

"Are you all right, Marcie?"

"No, I'm on edge. It's the thought of facing Mom and Dad, but it's also the detox shakes. I'm still recovering."

"You'll feel better once you're away from all this. You have to believe you're strong enough to beat it and you know you're not alone," Raven said.

"The bus for Gibsons, Sechelt and points north now boarding at Bay 23," the loudspeaker announced. The girls handed the bus driver their tickets and climbed on board.

"Let's sit at the back. I don't feel like being around other people right now," Marcie said.

Raven sat quietly looking out the window until they approached Horseshoe Bay. Marcie turned to her and asked, "Do you hate me?"

"Hate you! How could I hate you? You're my sister. I love you."

"Well, Mom and Dad must surely hate me after all I've put them through."

"Nobody hates you. We *all* love you. Why do you think I came to look for you? You will always be a part of our family. There's no rule that says you have to be perfect to belong to a family."

"But you're perfect."

"No I'm not — you're exaggerating."

"You always get the best grades, help Mom with the chores, give half of your money to help support the family. You even had the courage to come and look for me on skid row."

"That doesn't make me perfect — far from it. It's just that I set a goal for myself a long time ago. I decided then I wouldn't let anything stand in the way of my going to university. It's selfish, really, if you come right down to it, but it keeps me focused."

"But that's what I'm talking about. You had to use some of your hard-earned money for university to come and find me. I'm so sorry…" Marcie sobbed.

"Don't cry. You're worth every penny," Raven said as she hugged her sister.

"I'm scared to go home and face them."

"But they'll be so happy to see you. They might ground you until you're 75, but you'll survive," Raven laughed.

Marcie wiped away her tears and grinned. "I'm sure glad you're not handing out the punishment."

"Just because you and I don't make the same choices doesn't mean Mom and Dad love you less."

"What do you mean?"

"You are special in your own way. When you left home, it was as if the house was dimmer, missing your happy voice and laughter. I have always wished I was more like that."

"I *am* like you, in a way. I had dreams and goals too — of going to the city and being successful — but I didn't make it."

"As Dad always says, success is less important than learning from your mistakes. There's always next time."

"What do you mean 'next time'? I'm never going back there again."

"Not back to your old gang or the strip, but the city itself may still be the right place for you. Go to college. Get some skills. Do something you love. Find a roommate in a decent area. It doesn't even have to be Vancouver, there are other cities."

"It would take courage to go back. I have never been as frightened as I was these past few months. It was thrilling and addictive at first, but then it turned into a terrifying nightmare. The thought of dragging you into that world too...I'll never forgive myself."

"If you want to put it behind you, you can. Dad always said admitting a weakness is a strength in itself," Raven said as the bus boarded the ferry for home.

◆

Their father was there to meet them when they arrived at Earls Cove. He hugged them both and ushered them into the boat. He shouted above the drone of the boat's engine, "We'll talk in the morning." The girls knew that tomorrow there would be much to say, but for now their presence was enough.

◆

It was 8 a.m. and Marcie and her parents sat at the breakfast table. Tim and Allan had been pleased to see Marcie again, but quickly got caught up in plans for a tree fort and abandoned their cereal for the backyard. Raven was catching up on the schoolwork she'd missed and thought it best to leave her sister without an audience.

Marcie had practised several scenarios, but faced with the prospect of confessing all she could do was clear her throat.

Both parents looked at her expectantly. Finally, her father spoke. "I'd like to give thanks for Marcie's and Raven's safe return," he said softly. They joined hands and bowed their heads.

"Aren't you going to lecture me? Or ground me? Or something?" Marcie blurted.

"Have we ever lectured you?"

"No."

"Have we ever grounded you?"

"No."

"Then what makes you think we would now?"

"Well, I've changed. I've let you down."

"How have you let us down?"

"I…I hung out with a bad crowd. I did bad things."

"Are you hanging out with them anymore?"

"No."

"Are you still doing bad things?"

"No."

"Then it sounds to me as if you have changed for the better. Experiences don't have to make us bad as long as we grow from them," her father said.

"I didn't mean to hurt you," Marcie admitted with a sob.

Her mother smiled and stood up. She gathered her daughter in her arms and rocked her for a long time.

"When you have children of your own, you'll learn that pain is not a choice, it's part of loving and part of growing up. I remember when you were just learning to walk. I held your hand to keep you from falling, but eventually I knew you had to do it on your own. When you took your first independent steps, you were unsteady but determined. You're still that way," her mother said tenderly.

"Over the next days and weeks and months, there will be lots to tell us and you'll need help, professional help, help from the elders, and it will be hard. But for now we just want you to feel safe and to turn to us whenever you need to. Tomorrow I'm going to make a journey to Red Top. The mountain has always been a special place of sanctuary for our people, a spiritual place of healing. I was hoping you would come with me; we could leave at first light," her father offered.

EPILOGUE

Marcie had been calling regularly since she got back to Egmont two months ago, but J.L. wouldn't speak to her. She hoped this time he would agree to talk, that he would be in a better state of mind. Melissa answered.

"Hi, Melissa. How's he doing?"

"Well, his therapy is going well, but he's terribly depressed. He just mopes around the house. He won't talk to anyone."

"Did you tell him I called again?"

"Of course. I can't understand why he won't talk to you. He just keeps saying he doesn't want to be a burden."

"Tell J.L. I need his help. He's the only one who understands what I've been through and without him I'm afraid I might…. Just be sure to tell him, OK?"

"All right," Melissa said, a little unsure of herself.

When J.L. called back the next day, Marcie was so surprised she jumped in before he could say a word. "Listen closely, J.L. I don't want to hear any more about being a burden. I'm calling to tell you I bought a bus ticket to Kelowna and I'll be there tomorrow. I know there are jobs in the area and that your parents have a spare room I can rent. I can help you with your therapy and you can help me with mine — I'm still so shaky and I have horrible cravings. I need you, J.L. and my family knows how I feel about you. They've spoken to your parents and it's all set. I'm not asking your permission. I'm just warning you I'm landing on your doorstep," Marcie said before hanging up with a smile. Maybe they'd both found what they were looking for in the city after all — each other.

◆

Raven bounded down the stairs en route to the shed to fetch her supplies for the day's salal picking — she had some catching up to do to replace the money she'd spent during those days in the city. She felt more carefree than she had in days. Through the open window she breathed in the fragrant smell of the freshly cut cedar and heard the familiar *kwack, kwack* of the bird that was her namesake. On a tree branch just outside the window, the bluish purple glint of its feathers glistened in the sun. Suddenly, it took off, gliding across the blue sky with grace. Seconds later it was playing in the air currents — first a dive, then a spectacular roll

— before it settled back into the nest that it called home.

She turned toward the counter where she spotted an envelope addressed to her, written in a scrawl that looked vaguely familiar. Maybe Ben had finally responded to the letters she had sent care of Mr. Wilson's store. She tore open the envelope and pored over his note:

Dear Raven,

I don't know where to begin. Just after you left, Mr. Wilson made me an offer that would change all our lives. He said, because of his failing health and age, that he needed someone around the clock to help him with the business and his place. He wanted us to move into the house behind the bookstore — Robert and Anna too — and help out wherever we could. When I told the children we had a new home, they were so excited they could barely contain themselves and started packing their few belongings right away. Robert ran over and hugged Mr. Wilson so hard he started coughing. I couldn't stop grinning. But Anna had the strangest reaction. She sat with her eyes shut and recited, "I have just to shut my eyes, to go sailing through the skies, to go sailing far away...."

On our first night in Mr. Wilson's house, he went into the cupboard and brought out a large framed painting covered with a drop cloth. He

placed it on an easel stand, cleared his throat and
unveiled the picture.

"Look, it's the gown, the midnight-blue
crushed velvet one!" Anna shouted. Mr. Wilson
had found an old photo of Bertie in a newspaper
review of her performance and had hired an artist
to duplicate the photo for the portrait.

"Miss Bertie's spirit will be living here too,"
Mr. Wilson said, beaming.

Your friend forever,

Ben

P.S. Write me soon (I love having a real address!).

Acknowledgments

*The author would like to thank
Linda Topallian, SD#61 and the
Grade 6 and 7 classes of
Blanshard Elementary in Victoria.*

RESOURCES

BRITISH COLUMBIA RESOURCES

Carnegie Community Centre
Association
401 Main St.
Vancouver, BC
V6A 2T7
604-689-0397

Child Find BC
910 – 550 Victoria Street,
Prince George, BC
V2L 2K1
250-562-3463
Toll free: 1-888-689-3463
E-mail: childbcpg@aol.com

Child Youth and Family Advocate
600 – 595 Howe St.
Vancouver, B.C.
V6C 2T5
604-775-3203

Covenant House Vancouver
575 Drake St.
Vancouver, BC
V6B 4K8
604-685-7474
24 hour crisis centre:
604-685-7474

Downtown Eastside Residents'
Association
425 Carral St.
Vancouver, BC
V6B 6E3
604-682-0931

Downtown Eastside
Neighbourhood Safety Office
12 E Hastings
Vancouver, BC
V6A 1N1
604-687-1771

Downtown Eastside Youth Activities
Society
432 E Hastings
Vancouver, BC
V6A 1P7
604-251-3310

Downtown Eastside Women's
Centre
44 E Cordova
Vancouver, BC
V6A 1K2
604-681-8480
Legal Advocacy 604-681-4786
Women's phone 604-681-7458

Drug and Alcohol Counsellor
223 Main St.
Vancouver, BC
V6A 2S7
604-685-7300

Evelyn Saller Centre
320 Alexander St.
Vancouver, BC
V6A 1C3
604-665-3075

The Gathering Place
609 Helmcken St.
Vancouver, BC
V6B 5R1
604-665-2391

Innervisions Recovery Society
Men's Treatment Centre
837 Miller
Coquitlam, BC
V3J 4K7
604-939-1420

Needle Exchange Program
221 Main St.
Vancouver, BC
V6A 2S7
604-685-6561

**The Society for Children and Youth
of British Columbia**
3644 Slocan Street
Vancouver, BC
V5M 3E8
604-433-4180
E-mail: scy@portal.ca
Web site: http://www.scyofbc.org

**St. James Community Service
Society**
329 Powell
Vancouver, BC
V6A 1G5
604-606-0300

**Strathcona Adult Day Centre
Society**
105-400 Campbell
Vancouver, BC
V6A 3K2
604-251-6411

Strathcona Community Centre
601 Keefer St.
Vancouver, BC
V6A 3V8
604-713-1838

**Strathcona Community Mental
Health Team**
330 Heatley Ave.
Vancouver, BC
V6A 3G3
604-253-4401

**Vancouver Aboriginal
Friendship Centre Society**
1607 E Hastings
Vancouver, BC
V5L 1S7
604-251-4844

Youth Action Centre
342 E Hastings
Vancouver, BC
V6A 1P4
604-602-9747

The Odd Squad
c/o Vancouver Police Department
312 Main St.
Vancouver, BC
V6A 2T2
http://www.oddsquad.com

HELP LINES

AIDS/STD Information Line
604-872-6652
AIDS Vancouver Helpline
604-687-2437

Battered Women Support Services
604-687-1867

Cocaine Anonymous Vancouver
Hotline: (604) 662-8500
Web site: http://www.jlcl.com/ca

Help Line for Children
310-1234 (all area codes)

Mental Health Information Line
604-669-7600

Rape Crisis Centre
604-255-6344

Vancouver Crisis Centre
604-872-3311

**Youth against Gang Violence
and Youth Contact Line**
604-775-4264

**Women against Violence
against Women**
604-255-6344

OTHER RESOURCES

"Through A Blue Lens"
Veronica Mannix, director
Gillian Kovanic, producer, 1999
National Film Board of Canada
$39.95 institutions,
$19.95 individuals.
1-800-267-7710
Fax: 514-283-7564
http://www.nfb.ca

124 ◆ DIANE SILVEY

Being Aware, Taking Care
An information guide for parents,
counselors, youth agencies, teachers
and police addressing the dangers of
street life and exploitation of youth
in the sex trade.
ISBN 0-7726-2850-5

NATIONAL RESOURCES

**Alateen, a help line for families &
friends of alcoholics**
1-888-425-2666

**Alcohol and Drug Information and
Referral Service**
1-800-663-1441

Big Brothers and Sisters of Canada
113E – 3228 South Service Road,
Burlington, Ontario
L7N 3H8
905-639-0461
Toll free: 800-263-9133
E-mail: bbscmaster@aol.com

**Canadian Centre on Substance
Abuse**
300 – 75 Albert Street,
Ottawa, ON
K1P 5E7
613-235-4048
Web site: http://www.ccsa.ca

**Canadian Coalition for the Rights
of Children**
E-mail: ccrc@web.net
Web site:
http://www.rightsofchildren.ca

Child Find Canada
1-1808 Main Street
Winnipeg, MB
R2V 2A3
204-339-5584
Help line: 1-800-387-7962
E-mail: childcan@aol.com
Web site: http://www.childfind.ca

Save the Children Canada
300 – 4141 Yonge Street,
Toronto, ON
M2P 2A8
416-221-5501
E-mail: sccan@savethe children.ca
Web site:
http://www.savethechildren.ca

**ChildNet, your online guide to
youth and children resources**
Web site: http://www.child.net

The Child Welfare League of Canada
209 – 75 Albert Street,
Ottawa, Ontario
K1P 5E7
613-235-4412
E-mail: info@cwlc.ca
Web site: http://www.cwlc.ca

Cocaine Anonymous World Services
National Referral Line:
1-800-347-8998
E-mail: cawso@ca.org
Web site: http://www.ca.org

Kids Help Phone
1-800-668-6868
Web site: http://kidshelp.sympatico.ca

Operation Go Home
P.O. Box 53157
Ottawa, Ontario
K1N 1C5
613-230-4663
24-hour help line:
1-800-668-4663
E-mail: oghottawa@achilles.net
Web site:
http://www.operationgohome.ca

Parent Help Line
1-888-603-9100

Victims Information Line
1-800-563-0808

Violence Prevention Information
1-888-606-5483